parABnormal Magazine

December 2021

Edited by H. David Blalock

parABnormal Magazine
December 2021

All rights reserved. No part of this book may be reproduced or transmitted in any form or by any means, electronic or mechanical, including photocopying or recording or by any information storage and retrieval systems, without expressed written consent of the authors and/or artists.

parABnormal Magazine is a work of fiction. Names, characters, places, and incidents are products of the authors' imaginations. Any resemblance to actual events or persons, living or dead, is entirely coincidental.

Story and illustration copyrights owned by the respective authors and artists. *Evidence of the Eternal* appeared previously in *The Harrow* and **Eclectic Dreams**

Cover illustration "Agnesi Rime" © 2021 by Toe Keen
Cover design by Laura Givens
First Printing, December 2021
Hiraeth Publishing http://www.hiraethsffh.com/

Vol. III, No.4   December 2021
parABnormal Magazine is published quarterly on the 15th day of March, June, September, and December in the United States of America by Hiraeth Publishing, P.O. Box 1248, Tularosa, NM, 88352. Copyright 2021 by Hiraeth Publishing. All rights revert to authors and artists upon publication except as noted in selected individual contracts. Nothing may be reproduced in whole or in part without written permission from the authors and artists. Any similarity between places and persons mentioned in the fiction or semi-fiction and real places or persons living or dead is coincidental. Writers and artists guidelines are available online at www.hiraethsffh.com. Guidelines are also available upon request from Hiraeth Publishing, P.O. Box 1248, Tularosa, NM, 88352, if request is accompanied by a self-addressed #10 envelope with a first-class US stamp. Editor: H David Blalock.

Contents

Stories

8   A Ghostly Job by Karen Dent
32 The Great Harmonic Convergence by John Stratton
53 The Parapsychologist by Roger Lime
68 Mating Call by Kristi Petersen Schoonover
85 The Boy Who Drowned on Dry Land by Marlin Bressi
94 Evidence of the Eternal by Jonah Mason
102 Onorora by Daniel Paton
109 The Secret of the Dragon Cabinet by Malina Douglas

Poems

52 Grinning Death by Scott Coutourier
93 Breathers by Guy Belleranti
108 Silence, Solitude, and a Dark Night by Debasish Mishra
121 Ophiuchus by Januário Estevez

Articles

122 Russia's Well to Hell
125 Edison's Forgotten Spirit Phone

A Little Help, Please

In the world of the small indie press we fight a never-ending battle for attention to our work, as writers and in publishing. Here's an example: big publishers [you know who they are] have gobs of $$$ that they can devote to advertising and marketing. Here at Hiraeth Publishing, our advertising budget consists of the deposits for whatever soda bottles and aluminum cans we can find alongside the highways. Anti-littering laws make our task even more difficult . . . ☺

That's where YOU come in. YOU are our best promoter. YOU are the one who can tell others about us. Just send 'em to our website, tell them about our store. That's all. Just that.

Of course, we don't mind if you talk us up. We're pretty good, you know. We have some award-winning and award-nominated writers and artists, plus other voices well-deserving to be heard [not everyone wins awards, right?] but our publications are read-worthy nevertheless.

That number once again is:

www.hiraethsffh.com

Friend us on Facebook at Hiraeth Publishing

Follow us on Twitter at @HiraethPublish1

What???

No subscription to parABnormal Magazine??

We can fix that . . .

Just go here and order:

https://www.hiraethsffh.com/product-page/parabnormal-magazine-subscription

*...also makes a great gift
any time of the year*

The Wolves of Glastonbury
by Edward Cox & Terrie Leigh Relf

What happens in Glastonbury stays in Glastonbury—even if it means the end of one of humanity's longest alternate lifelines. The hunt is on for Claire and Ethan . . .

https://www.hiraethsffh.com/product-page/wolves-of-glastonbury-by-terrie-leigh-relf-edward-cox

A Word from the Editor

Welcome once again to the boundary of the possible, the improbable, and the mysterious.

As 2021 comes to a close, there is hope the world is climbing out of a deep hole and back into the sunlight of health. The last two years have been hard for many, worse for some. We hope the next year will be better.

Now, back to business.

In this issue, we see the first in a series of stories by Karen Dent, tales of an unusual ghost hunter and her assistant. We look forward to seeing more of these tales from Karen and her sister Roxanne and hope you enjoy them.

We try to present stories of various ilk to meet the tastes of the variety of our readers from around the globe. We accept excellent work not just from the United States, but from Europe, Africa, Australia, and Asia because talent is not found in only one place. We hope to be able to continue to receive submissions from everywhere the written word and art are appreciated and created.

So. We have a story about becoming a psychic, or at least seeming to, and the after effects. Following on, there is an interesting story about the revenge of the avians over generations. We then look at how a birthmark connects people in a less than wonderful way. The answer to the question of the mystery of the dragon cabinet comes next.

Lastly, we present two articles for your information and entertainment, one about Russia's well to Hell and the other about Edison's spirit phone.

As always, I invite you to let us know what you think about the magazine. Drop us a note at parabnormal.magazine@gmail.com. We look forward to hearing from you.

H. David Blalock
December 2021

A Ghostly Job
Karen Dent

I won't say the severed head that rolled into my kitchen like a bowling ball didn't make me jump. I yelped, ran a hand through my short, dark curly hair and studied the object at my feet. The bone-dry, bloodless state, made it look more like a rubber Halloween mask than a dead, human one. I gave a sharp, reproving glance at the open door, but my ghost didn't bother entering yet.

"Percival, not funny."

"Ooooh," Percy's disembodied voice intoned, "but I think it is, bwahahahahaaa."

I picked up the head. A hefty weight, I stared into its eyes and studied the face: flabby jowls, faded ice-blue eyes, a squashed nose which had been broken several times in a hard lifetime of disappointments. Thin lips with deep marionette lines that tracked from the corners of the mouth and ended at the jaw of a weak chin.

I ran my hand over his bald pate. Like insect antennae, two long, skinny hairs stuck out from the pale, pink wasteland. I raised my voice, "What's his crime?"

A soft voice next to my ear made me jump, "Ugly doesn't need a crime."

I waved my hand through icy air and sucked my teeth. "You're too old for that."

"I enjoy seeing you unsettled. Makes the innards I don't have, all warm and jolly." Percy coalesced into his favorite form, a 16th century Musketeer.

"Keep it up and I'll request another partner. At which point you will spend the rest of your conscious, bored life surrounded by the white-on-white décor of the Great Abyss."

"Pitiful. You are devoid of fun." He glided to my windows.

I carried the head over to my faux fireplace. "Yes, I'm a black hole of responsibility when it comes to collecting. What's his story?"

"To choose a bitter and cruel life. A man who was dead

inside. At the end he sold his soul to feel anything."

"And the demon?"

Percy gracefully kicked out his right leg, "Booted back to whence he came." He took a grand, flourishing bow.

I pushed a fireplace brick and a door swung open with a whoosh. I stepped into a narrow space that was 'in-between'.

Designed with floor to ceiling shelving, it held an array of soulless heads in various shapes, sizes and disgruntled expressions.

I continued, "Despite their transgressions, it's disrespectful to treat them like objects."

"Humph."

I carefully wiped off the face and gently pressed the two hairs back into place before I placed it on a bottom shelf. I looked around and took inventory. Almost full. *Enough room for just one more.* I didn't realize how successful Percy and I had been.

I slowly returned to the living room,

Percy glided over to my couch and flopped dramatically with his booted feet upon my coffee table, "What enthralling vision shall we watch tonight?"

He settled in, his form becoming more substantial, the colors more vivid. The cushions beneath his back and buttocks dipped as he gathered mass.

He glanced at me. With that movement his hat and plummy feathers, waved. "As you know, I am quite struck by your 'Game of Thrones' however," his hand shot up to stop me lest I protest, "if you prefer something new tonight I am, as you are aware, flexible and open to suggestion."

I snorted.

He turned his attention to the television and tried to grab the remote.

It remained untouchably remote to his energies. I refrained from mentioning the irony.

He shrugged, sat back and continued to stare at the television screen. "We of course would need at least one segment of that glorious tee-vee program, then whatever you wish...within reason." He turned, "Why so quiet?" Alarmed, he floated up. "Are you well?"

"I am quite well. I've just now realized we have but one more collection to gather before you...before sentence is passed."

He stiffened. "A mere bauble of unimportance. I am quite prepared. Now, please pick up that blasted thing, point and shoot at the magic window." He gallantly bowed and gestured at the couch, "After you, m'Lady."

I stayed where I was. "We need to discuss our strategy Percival. This is one of the times we do it together."

He brushed imaginary crumbs from his shirt front. My apprentice had once been a demon-possessed-human who agreed to a plea bargain of sorts and was engaged in a new Program. Hopefully a successful one, where corrupted human could work off the smut on their souls. Time in the abyss gave many an opportunity to re-think their choices.

For most of our two years together, Percy amused me. Now I was annoyed.

"A cavalier attitude is not called for. I don't want you to become corrupted again."

"Pfff." He waved me off and sat back on the couch. His body looked relaxed but I could see his little tells of tension. His right hand was now missing a finger and his hat sported no feather.

"Percival," I began, "as spirit coalesced to serve a greater purpose, you are still vulnerable. You can no longer lose your body, but your spirit is still at risk. If you had not agreed to our arrangement, your head would still be sitting on another Reaper's shelf." He looked away. "Do you remember what that was like?"

"I do indeed," he said quietly. "With great sorrow."

"Then we need to talk about this last collection before you go before the Board. The important one. The final —"

"Yes, yes. THE One." He looked at the ceiling, "The most important and most hazardous."

I added, "And with a greater chance of my own demise —"

He leapt up and brandished his sword, "M'Lady, I am prepared to meet and vanquish evil incarnate." Both eyebrows rose as he added, "After all, I was married once."

I laughed. "An oldie but goodie."

"Oldie? I just made it up myself. Right now, on the spot." He materialized a quill pen, a scroll of parchment and ink well. "I must put it down or it will be lost forever." He wrote furiously. The ink well and scroll hovered beneath his hand.

I sighed, went to my desk and touched the small crystal skull sitting upon my mundane bills. A light fired deep within its eye sockets and a booming voice rippled through the room.

"YES?"

Percy jumped and spilled ink over his parchment. "Damnable woman. I would consider it a blessing if you let me know when you planned communication."

I ignored him. "Ianna and Percival need immediate information about our next and last collection."

Percival glided over and stood next to me.

"You already have the information needed to proceed. The Device will display who and where."

"That was never the plan," I said annoyed. "We cannot rely on the poor information available in this time space continuum."

"You must. It has been decreed."

"What? By whom? Show me the paperwork."

"None available."

"I wish to speak to a higher source."

"Not possible."

"Don't be ridiculous. We need assistance. The Board might not fully support this project, but you cannot abandon us to the possibility of failure."

Percival muttered, "Cowards," and jabbed his rapier at the skull.

"That is the ruling. End of Communication."

Light faded from the skull. I touched it again, then roughly manhandled it for several seconds waiting for re-animation. Frustrated, I slammed it down.

"Ye Gods Lady, I never noticed what large hands you have. Gigantic for one so petite."

I glared at him and he backed away.

"Take no offense. A good thing back in my day. Excellent for kneading bread."

"Focus, Percy. Did you not hear?"

"I have ears."

"Apparently just to keep your hat on." I stalked around the room. "They can't just cut us off like that. That was never part of the deal."

Percy put an arm around my shoulders. "Perhaps not part of your deal. I am full of sorrow for I believe this is my test more so than yours."

His cold settled across my neck, down my shoulders and I shivered. It was not unpleasant, but still I moved away from his offer of comfort.

"No, Percy, this is not of your doing."

"Oh, I disagree. It is my task. It is my burden to seek out and capture the foolish human who allows this most vile demon to consume his soul. I have given you my pledge." He raised his fist and crossed his chest. "To Reap the Corrupted Who Could Not Be Saved. Send Back to Hell Those Who Lead Them Astray." He bowed, then smiled. "I also recall you offered your own word and life that those of us who were savable, would be. I, and several others are most grateful. Truly."

I felt betrayed and abandoned. "The council never said they would withdraw their support at time of gravest danger."

"No," he paused, "but it is fitting."

"How so?"

"They are divided in their wishes for you and the few others who have chosen this new path of dealing with evil. Some hope the old ways of punishment to be restored. If I fail, it will be yet more proof they are right. If you perish, reason to halt the program."

I thought about that. A few other Reapers like me, the watchers and guardians of this world, had become tired of the never-ending battle with evil. What was the point if we could not stem the tide? Stop the corruption before it completely poisoned its human host? If we could do that and banish each demon from Earth, would that not be worth a try? A way to heal the humans who allowed Demons to suckle upon their souls.

I did my homework on Percival before I made my

commitment. I believed in my companion/servant. And while he had the ability to disappoint, he proved over and over again, he was undauntingly good. His one and only mistake brought him to this crossroad.

I dropped on the couch. "This new development on the last leg of our journey makes no sense. I fear for you."

"And I for you."

"Me?"

He sat beside me. "Sadly I am most keenly aware that temptation to choose evil over goodness is far more difficult than one thinks. However..."

"Go on."

"Two collections ago, we had a fully realized demon in human skin with skill to twist any judgment within earshot. A skin sack that smiled and said words without truth."

"I remember. A natural politician rising to power."

"I was not swayed. Though Kings and Queens have been corrupted by lesser Demons, you hoped his words were true."

I shrugged. "Initially, his message was about love."

"A most powerful motivator. Many battles are fought in its name. Many betrayals. Many misunderstandings."

"Your point?"

"I go to battle alone. You can –"

"Absolutely not," I said loudly. "I can embrace an idea without being blinded by the source. I know love can hide reason and right by being wrongly placed." I added softly, "Your lesson, not mine."

He turned back to the television. "Let us dwell upon this later. Now we watch your magic screen for it tells us true of loyalty, love, betrayal, and greed."

I picked up the channel changer. "Where do you think the characters in Game of Thrones could have chosen better?"

He smiled. "That would change the telling of the tale and what fun would that be?"

***

The next morning, I staggered out to a cold kitchen where Percy paced. "Finally! It's quite vexing to watch you waste time sleeping."

I ignored him and turned on my coffee maker.

"You see," he stepped next to me, "I've been formulating a plan. Madame, we must trust each other to bring this Evil Doer down."

I heard the whistle of his blade behind me, felt the wind. He was getting really good with manifesting the physical. "Give me peace for at least 30 minutes."

"Time is of the essence. I believe this demon, Azzubuzeti, deals in betrayals. Of trusts broken. Of greed. We must let Azzubuzeti think I have not changed. That I have been plotting, biding my time and would betray you for my heart's desire."

Odd. Percy never mentioned a demon's name. I yawned and glanced at him. "Would you betray me?"

"Never." A dark look crossed his face as I turned back to preparing my coffee. "You do realize," he insisted, "a heart's desire can be a tempting thing. Think upon it." He sidled up to me. "You lead a cloistered life. Nothing but work and collections." He leaned in and whispered in my ear, "There is much to enjoy elsewhere."

Percy never invaded my space. And he never, ever whispered in my ear. Alarms blared. I turned and looked into his eyes.

Someone else looked back.

In less than a micro-second, my skin tightened against my bones, my lips stretched into a snarl and from my chest, boomed a Command.

"*Get Out!*"

The sound thundered against the walls of my kitchen and cracked its plaster. The clock shattered and fell to the floor.

Black sooty air leached from Percy. The stink of sulfur burned my nose. Then it was gone and the kitchen was warm again.

Percy, bedraggled and limp, stood before me. I kicked a chair under his swaying legs before he collapsed in a heap, fell through, and sprawled onto the floor.

"What just happened? he asked.

"You were possessed. Quick, what do you remember

before it happened?"

"Prior to being possessed? I am a Wraith. How does a Wraith become possessed?"

"Think!"

"Stop yelling, Shrew!"

Like a drunkard who fell and couldn't quite make it upright, Percy staggered to his feet, teetered here and there before he straightened. He yanked his waistcoat down, took his hat off and fluffed the feathers avoiding eye contact.

"My apologies for calling you a Shrew. My head felt as detached as our friends in your secret room." He gently touched his neck before he finally looked at me. "I thought perhaps you abandoned your promise and used your sabre to end my time prematurely."

My eyebrows rose. I knew betrayal was a major issue of his but I thought we crossed that trust barrier a while ago. "I told you on my honor I would not do that." He stayed silent. "I have faith in you Percival."

"Yes, well, circumstances change, dear Lady, and I for one would not have blamed you."

I smiled. "A ghost possessed. That's a new one." We were quiet for a minute before I said, "Do you remember anything before you lost your sense of self?"

He shook his head.

I pressed, "It might have been the demon we're seeking. Did you mention Its name while I was sleeping? Think about the good ol' days?"

Percy looked away.

"Nothing before It moved in?"

Percy stiffened, "Your harping does bring something to mind." Silent, he brooded.

"For cripes sake Percy, what was it? If It can get into your thoughts and use it to invade your ectoplasm, I need to know what you were thinking."

He floated over to the sink, turned, and managed to look shifty. "Nothing out of the ordinary. Sword play. Vanquishing resistance with my incredible abilities." He bowed stiffly and headed to the door. "I must retreat before I cause further harm."

"What?" I followed him. "Don't' be ridiculous –" He melted into a swirling, riot of colors. "Percy!"

Frustrated, I returned to the living room and flopped onto the couch. *The entity that embodied Percy for that small window of time was chillingly realistic. How did it manage such a swift and undetected transition? Unless somehow -- Percy allowed it.*

***

When he returned, he still wouldn't share what allowed the demon access to his spirit. "No, good Lady, I will not tell. But rest assured it will not happen again."

I was not assured. But no amount of nagging, badgering, or threatening got me an answer. I couldn't extract what I wanted because I promised personal privacy when we forged our working relationship. Unless it related to the job, I couldn't compel him to tell me. In retrospect, a stupid promise.

Three nights away October 31 would roll around. Halloween thinned the veil between demon and earth. It allowed bigger predators to squeeze through the rift and walk amongst humans. It also allowed me to spot them easier. Their dark smudge upon the space around them was luminescent. I called it their 3-E's; Emanating-Evil-Energy. Fortunately, the typical human sensed them and moved away.

Unfortunately, the 3-E's magnetized people filled with anger, hate, and misery. Riots, fights, and brutal murder was never far behind their appearance.

For the first time in a hunt, I was apprehensive.

***

"Azzubuzeti is not the name of the demon we are seeking," Percy told me.

"I didn't think it was." Knowing an actual demon name is powerful and a dangerous threat to the one exposed. "So, why do you think It told you it was?"

"A rival to be gotten rid of. An unpleasant joke, or It expected us to place our focus there." He looked at me. "Tis unfortunate It now knows your strength."

I smiled. "Not quite."

He shivered. "My God, woman, most unpleasant when

you expose your teeth like that."

"Time to begin." I walked to the television and turned it on. A bright faced newscaster sat at a desk with his cheerful co-anchor beside him. I fiddled at the back of the set where I'd attached my Location Device. Electricity from the television assisted with its fine tuning.

Percy materialized a pen, parchment, and sat on the edge of the couch. "Perhaps your mysterious box will show us more than what they look like and a good, solid place where we can pounce and destroy. It has in the past."

"We'll see."

We still ran the risk of being seen and caught for killing someone who was already dead. Well, dead in the spiritual sense. Banishment of the demon had to occur at the same time otherwise it could wiggle free to inhabit and corrupt another poor soul.

So far, Percy had done well alone. And on the difficult cases we worked together, we had back-up and intel that assisted us in both Reaping and Banishment.

My hand fiddled with the finger divots and smelled burnt ozone. The smooth Device felt warm and greasy, like a living thing. I quickly activated it and wiped my hand on my jeans. It never felt right to touch the Device and I repressed a shiver.

The screen flickered and went dark. Grey and white roiling swirls undulated and showed nothing but the curtain before the fourth dimension.

I joined Percy on the couch. We waited.

Three minutes passed before a word appeared.

WICKED.

The first clue always relates to a place. I frowned. I'd never known the device to make a judgment on a location. A nest of thieves? Murderers? A wicked den of despots?

I let it go and waited for the next clue.

There was a loud buzz, a strobe-like flicker, then nothing. When the next clue came in, the grey sea flickered, sparked, and appeared to cut off half the word

...*SEX*

...sparks again, then

...*HILL.*

17

Percy leaned in eagerly. "A bordello on a hill?"

"For heaven's sake, Percival. Half words could mean anything and be anywhere."

The screen darkened then showed us the grainy face of our quarry.

We both stiffened. A jolly, roly-poly face appeared laughing at something. A twinkle in its eyes, a mischievous expression and...braces on its teeth. Young. Maybe ten?. The screen sparked again, made a low buzz, and went dead-black. We turned to each other.

Percy shook his head. "That cannot be who we seek." The quill and paper vanished. "I do not help to reap children."

"Nor do I."

"Then why show that face? Was it a mistake?"

"I don't know. The Device obviously had interference projecting information. Perhaps the picture was meant to show the person the child was laughing at."

"It better." Percy stuck his chin out and crossed his arms.

"Let's sift through the clues and see what we come up with before judgment. If the interference was deliberate and meant to lead us astray, good. Let whoever did it, think they were successful."

Percy perked up. "Good plan."

The television popped back to the news channel. I turned it off. We sat in silence for a while before I got up and walked to my wall map. Our territory for Reaping was within the five New England states; New Hampshire, Rhode Island, Massachusetts, Vermont, and Maine. I felt no pull to any of them.

Something about the word "wicked" tickled my memory. I let it go and tested Percy. "What are the clues supposed to give us?"

"The first is the Naming Word. Therefore, *Wicked* must be the name of the house, tavern, blacksmith, or church where both human and demon reside."

"Good. The other clues had pieces missing, only half words. What do we know about those?"

"They show where the evil doers hide."

"Exactly. They narrow our parameters; street, city, county." I turned back to my map. "So we look to see how and where those three half-words lead us."

He rubbed his hands. "S.E.X. This should be a most enjoyable search."

I ignored him and headed to my laptop, typed in our hunting grounds with the last letters of *SEX*. Massachusetts had the most promising clues with Middlesex and Essex counties and various streets called Essex. I decided to narrow my search there when I remembered "wicked" is used as an adjective, 'Wicked good', 'Wicked fun', and noun like 'Wicked Yoga'. When I puzzled in Sex and Hill, I smiled.

Wicked Large B&B, on Essex Street, in Haverhill.

***

"Percy."

The car remained silent. My companion, scrunched into a fetal position in the back, grunted.

"If we don't know what It looks like, we are vulnerable. If we discount the child, we are vulnerable."

He slowly unfolded in a colorful expression of red and orange rage. "I will not be responsible for sending a child into the Great Abyss." He oozed forward and dropped into the passenger seat.

I repressed my inclination to chop his cold air into little bits. "You are supposed to keep a sharp and open mind on the job."

"I do."

"Really?" I glanced at him. "Have you considered the image could have been an illusion and showed us what the human looked like as a child?" Percy was silent. "Especially if they knew your prejudices."

Percy cursed. "Blast all demons and their trickster ways."

"I need your entire focus on this job. Whatever pans out. Am I clear?"

After several seconds and much fading in and out, Percy pronounced, "I am yours to command." A moment passed before he added, "Do we know more of the second demon? It sounds like Lyesmith." He looked at me. "Loki the troublemaker?"

"What?" The car swerved.

"There are two who we seek." He turned to me. "The one who visited me in your kitchen, and another linked to that one."

"You know this how?"

"I sensed It briefly before I, um passed out."

"Are you telling me we are to Reap and Banish two Demons and Human Souls?"

"Yes."

I drove in silence.

Percy patted my shoulder. "Don't be discouraged. I know a bit more than the average previously possessed."

"Oh?"

"Yes. I don't believe you are aware of how much information I hold regarding knowledge of the dark."

I tightened my grip on the wheel. "Tell me."

"In the down below, some of those cursed align with another for control. They believe this will give them power to widen the rift. Of course, it always ends poorly for the weaker Demon since they are consumed. The stronger adds to their influence along with a few curses the weaker one spews before they disappear."

I slowed down and pulled the car to the curb. "The Council is aware of their plots and obsessions. Do you have new information?"

Percy fidgeted. "I do."

"Because of your close ties?"

"Not entirely."

I soul gazed and saw a bit of smut still on his aura, but that was to be expected. My gut clenched. "Have you been communing with the demon world, Percival?"

He let out a huff of air. "Not really. I –"

"Stop. There is no 'not really' with demons. You know that."

"Damn it, woman, let me continue. Very vexing to have you interrupt when I speak. I lose concentration." He sniffed. "It takes a great deal to keep up my visage."

He harrumphed and managed to re-coalesce while I took note of the missing buckles to his boots and the absence of his rakish eyebrow perpetually lifted in amusement.

Finally, he sat back and stroked his pointed beard. "My connection with my corruptor was severed when I was sent to the Great Abyss. However, on my way out, I stole a book."

"A book?"

"Well, of course there was no physical book since it would burst into flame before it left, but the information didn't. Just one volume of many from the demon archives."

"Keep going."

"As you know I am quite the Bard,"

"The book," I gritted out. "What. Did. It. Say?"

He cleared his throat. "I have quite a gift of remembering songs, if nothing else, so I made up little ditty's connecting the words." He looked at me, "Isn't that clever?"

"Is there a lyric that will help us right now?"

He sang quietly:

"To wrest the power from demons bonded
'Take thee long, to see and ponder
Has one or the t'other swallowed It's own?
Then sacrificed an innocent, with a mother's bone."

He beamed and waited for my approval.

"What the hell does that mean?".

He glared. "You are naught but a Scold and sour Wench. Why should I know? You're the Reaper."

We sat in silence. He had a point. I should know. The Board should know. Probably did but chose not to pass on the information. This lack of support, which I now believed was deliberate obstruction, was unsettling.

A nibble of paranoia made me wonder if someone at the top had been corrupted. I shook off the thought but planned to circle back once our job was done.

Percival's ability to remember a book brought from the demon world was extraordinary. How many other souls have bits and pieces we could use to close and tighten the veil?

Of course, it would be helpful if we could interpret the meaning. A demon's twisted way of thinking made it nearly impossible to decipher.

I looked at Percival staring out at the night, humming to himself. A companion/servant who was saved might have a different perspective. But would dwelling on the words lead them into danger of losing their soul again?

"All right. I need to understand what you know I don't. Am I correct in assuming we are going into battle with two demons and two humans to Banish and Reap?"

Percy smiled crookedly. "A challenge worthy of my redemption."

"Tell me what you think the passage means but," I stressed, "don't think too hard."

Percy sat back. A guitar materialized across his chest which he plucked. "I do believe it means we seek a woman, a mother who would be the corrupted and corruptor. Does that make sense?" He added, "I do not know if we seek the child, but I feel relief."

I did not.

***

Wicked Large B&B was a thin brownstone centered in the Town of Haverhill. Night activity rippled up and down the street. Cigarette smoke billowed, bursts of laughter and colorful language peppered the sidewalk. The unseasonably warm evening encouraged outside seating where the clink of glasses and murmur of love floated along the airwaves.

None of which penetrated the narrow space in front of our building. A dead zone, where the picture window revealed a cute Bistro within.

"Appears a charming establishment," Percy said. "Shall we?"

When we entered, we cloaked ourselves; one Normal and a gust of air.

Wicked Large was of course, exceedingly small. Dim and shadowy, the gourmet restaurant barely seated 20. The brick walls held large colorful posters of 1920's Paris, illusion spoiled by black mold that curled the corners.

Percy muttered, "A busty serving wench would help cheer this place up."

According to their website, the Bed section of Wicked had two guest rooms on the second floor. The dour faced Hostess rushed over and squeezed out a smile.

She glanced at my overnight bag. "You must be Ms. Harvester. Room first or dinner?"

"Dinner."

"Anyone joining you?" She looked hopefully behind me.

"No".

She grabbed a menu and beelined to my table.

My Google search told me this was a family-run business. The Proprietor, busy at the cash box, the wife guarding the door, and three children who roamed the room taking orders. Their children, one female, 25 the other 14 and one boy about 11 who looked sickly.

Percy whispered. "There. Do you see him?"

"Hard not to, Sir Obvious."

"A sharp tongue can whittle friendship to a thin stick," he muttered.

"Shhh."

The boy approached with a breadbasket. "Can I get you anything?"

"Yes. I'd like ..." I let my sentence dangle.

"Yes?" He smiled, revealing braces.

A willing offer is an open invitation to ask questions that MUST be answered. I leaned forward and whispered. "Who are you?"

A glazed look crossed his face, "Milo Stratton, son of Dominick Stratton." He tried to leave.

"Stay," I said firmly. He stopped and stood staring at us with a blank look.

All eyes stared at my table. I picked up the menu, pointed at something and smiled. "Who of your family is not...the same?"

"My mother."

"Thank you. You may go."

I turned to Percy and said behind the menu. "He is merely enthralled. Are you happy?"

"Exceedingly. Yet..."

"Yet?"

"Do you not feel It? The other puppeteer is here and is stronger," he indicated the Hostess, "than his mother."

Involved in shielding my questions, I'd stopped allowing my senses full awareness.

A cold, bitter, despair hit me like an anvil. The same that blossomed and permeated the sidewalk. I looked at the other diners and felt a huge frieze of fear.

Faces morphed, teeth gleamed, the demon grinned out at us from each face before it said in unison.

"Welcome."

I threw a fireball of paralysis at the room while Percy tossed one of forgetful to protect the patron's sanity. All slumped forward into their minestrone and steak pizzaiola. All except the girls who vanished and the boy who disappeared into the kitchen.

I began a locating spell. The demon thread led off with the boy, except it was weak.

I watched Percy stalk to the Hostess. He leaned down and began to whisper. She squirmed and tried to slither away from his lips. Her ears turned scarlet, then smoked. She screamed, a high, pitched whine that shattered glassware. She shuddered and stilled. Percy rose, removed his rapier, sliced off her head, and began the Reaping Ritual.

I closed my eyes and concentrated. Strong demon energy emanated from the basement. I hate basements. Earthen floored, dank and dark, it's always the beginning of demon summoning.

Being their point of entrance, it was difficult to cage them there. Especially so because their escape back to their world was so handy.

Dealing with two manifestations of evil, I could guarantee there would be more than one sliding door home.

I followed the boy into the kitchen and saw him quivering behind a rolling cart. Tears streaked his dirty face. I felt pity.

Until he lunged with a butcher knife.

I knocked the weapon away and felt Milo's teeth snap

down viciously on my forearm. Metal braces ripped at my flesh, teeth worried skin. I screamed and tried to yank my arm away.

Like a dog with a chew toy, he swung with it, teeth and jaws clamped in place. I looked down at his grimy face and saw the demon who had escaped Percy, grinning back. I smiled and leaned in.

"*STAY*," I Commanded and watched the Demon's eyes change from glee to fear. It released Its hold and tried to disappear.

Milo's jaw relaxed. He dropped to the floor and vomited, choking on my blood.

I grabbed his hair and yanked his head up. The Demon looked back at me, eyes wet, pupils dilated with panic.

"Milo Stratton, son of Dominick Stratton, I release you. This Demon no longer controls your body. I Banish –"

The Demon sobbed. "Wait!" then grabbed my bitten arm and squeezed.

I yelled and tossed him. He thumped to the floor and I heard a sickening sound. The knife's sharp blade sliced deep into Milo's abdomen. The Demon chuckled.

I flipped Milo over, removed the blade and pressed my hand upon his stomach. "*SLEEP A BLESSED SLUMBER. REPAIR.*"

I stared directly into the Demon's eyes. "Fool. I let go of the body but not my Command. You cannot leave."

Realizing it was trapped, the Demon howled.

"I Banish You To Nothing. I Banish You To Nowhere. I Banish You –"

"Noooooo,"

"—To The Void."

The kitchen was silent except for the steady drip of my blood. My arm throbbed. I checked Milo. His blood barely oozed from his wound. None of his vital organs were compromised so I left him where he was. I would call 911 when Percy and I were done.

"Percival?" I called as I got up and cradled my arm.

Percy floated in and saw my wound. "Do you need assistance?"

"Later."

He looked down at Milo. "Stupid Demon possessed the boy?"

I nodded. "Caught and banished. What about her?"

He held up the head. "She saw the error of her ways. Might be a candidate for your program." He paused. "She is not the mother we seek. The true mother, the Trickster is below." He strode past me. "We must hurry. Her plans include elevation and more death."

***

Wooden steps led into a classic horror film. Blood-soaked walls, written spells etched into dried blood, the smell of a slaughterhouse with the fine undercurrent of sulfur.

Nothing ever changed in pursuing Demons.

Percival pressed close. I welcomed his chill as we descended into a hot and sticky basement. I whispered, "What else do you know?"

"The older daughter was young when she birthed Milo." A beat. "The blood you see, is her newly born child used as a sacrifice." I heard him swallow. "She will not be remorseful."

I shuddered. We now knew the kind of magic used to enhance the demon's power and we were afraid. A mother who offered her innocent babe's blood and life to Evil would gain much. It allowed the triangulation of power to flow easily from Demon to Human to Demon. It was one of the most powerful and hardest spells to break.

We continued to descend. I asked softly, "Do you have any idea what she asked as payment?"

A cracked, scratchy voice came from the darkness. "Why don't you just ask me?"

A numbing cold passed through my bones. I shook myself and saw the older daughter by a makeshift altar. Glowing, 3-E energy undulated from her body. I cursed myself for forgetting demons can cloak their energy as well as I can. Tethered in both worlds, they can wax and wane. With one exception.

Some demons to gain ultimate power, will deliberately sever ties with their world. Stronger here, they are also vulnerable. If caught and banished, they have nowhere to go but to death's big sleep. I really hoped this fiend was one of those arrogant bastards.

"Are you afraid to talk to me, oh Mighty Reaper and her Minion?" The voice was a vibrato that chilled. It echoed with all the human souls it consumed.

Something squirmed on the Altar behind the woman. The young sister. Percy stiffened beside me.

"Why give up so much?" I asked.

She laughed a throaty, rich contralto. "So much? Look around you. A slave to servitude? No. I am ready to ascend." Arms wide she gestured around her. "I will have a life that will never end. Eternity with just one more sacrifice."

Percy rushed into the basement and swung his sword. "Evil incarnate get thee–" he hunched over, started to choke and dropped his sword.

"Shut up, ridiculous ghost."

Percy lifted his head and wheezed, "Ghost? I am spirit with a soul you blot upon –"

"Silence, Apparition." She waved a hand and Percival disappeared.

"Percy!" I started forward and almost fell. My feet tangled in wire stretched across the steps. I grabbed the slimy wall and righted myself.

The Demon chuckled. "Fear for yourself, Reaper. Not for the gust of air who has no substance." She cocked her head. "What? No command words for me?"

We both knew they would not work on someone who had no humanity left in their body.

A sickly green light appeared above the altar. The child beneath it stopped struggling.

The woman grinned. She held an ancient, bone knife in her hand and waved it. "Care to save my sister, Reaper? An innocent who will join my bounty of souls."

Her laugh was a cacophony of voices. Their screams "Save me!" hurt my heart.

I stayed where I was as she glided to the Altar and stared down at her sister. She raised her hand.

I cleared my throat. "Do it, Percy."

She whirled around and stared at me. "Why speak to

your servant who is not here?" Fear threaded the words.

If Percy didn't do what he had to, we were all lost.

Silently he appeared behind the possessed woman. A Reaper knife held high above his head, he stabbed down.

She screamed before she crumpled inelegantly onto the filthy floor.

The Demon escaped seconds before the knife severed Its Host's spinal cord and thus, Its connection.

"Bye," It taunted as It darted into the ceiling and disappeared. Laughter echoed throughout the room.

Frustrated, I realized It wasn't as arrogant as we thought and still kept a way home.

Percy whispered into the fallen woman's ear while I rushed to the young sister tied to the altar. Her glassy eyes stared at nothing. Naked and unresponsive, I untied her bonds and tried to sit her up. Dead weight. I slapped her face a few times. "Come on baby, focus."

I heard Percy say, "Damnable woman, you must listen to me."

She issued a sharp bark of laughter before she wretched up blood. "Stupid Reaper. Whatever you did to my body, my Lord will fix. Don't you know I am no longer mortal?"

Percy and I looked at each other.

"Time to go," I said.

I positioned the still catatonic teen to the edge of the Altar and readied to hoist her over my shoulder Fireman Style. Tears gathered in her eyes and I bent in. "Trust me. Everything will be –"

The revolting odor of decay, rot and spoiled meat blew out from her mouth. Her eyes rolled back and I stared into a black and malevolent Hell.

Hands snapped around my throat. Stone-hard fingers squeezed my neck. Instinctively, I tugged at them while tiny specks exploded across my vision. Tidal waves of blood thundered in my ears.

My telescoped vision saw her face draw near. Drool spilled from her open mouth. Snapping jaws drew close.

She was going to eat my face.

I stopped clawing at the fingers of death and punched

her. The delicate snap of her nose bone brought a gush of blood from both nostrils. The vice-like grip softened which gave me a moment to suck in air and gasp,

"*RELEASE. STAY.*" The Commands boomed and rocketed around the room.

Simultaneously, the young girl's hands fell from my neck. I gazed at her and knew her mind and soul were elsewhere.

That didn't stop the Demon from raging within her body. We watched the surface of her skin ripple, curses etched in her belly, monster faces stretched and leered from her chest and abdomen.

"*BE STILL.*" I further Commanded.

The fury subsided, eyes calculating.

I cursed myself for being tricked. The Demon did abandon Its home world to gain power here and only had a tiny window of time once Its connection was severed, to find another corrupted soul and body to possess with walls in place to shield against my Commands.

With no portal home and denied It's primary Host's body, the only one available to possess was the sacrificial sister. An innocent who is possessed, is a weak vessel.

She became the cage we snapped shut upon the Demon.

I heard a death rattle. The cause of all this grief lay in a pool of blood. Mouth agape, the souls she'd captured floated out, up, and winked away.

***

The Demon suffered Its final death. The opened rift was sealed. The damage it did to the soul of Tanya was hard to accept. We should have known about her corruption before it was too late. Why didn't we? Good question that needed answers.

Today, Percy is going before the Board. I had no doubt he would be issued another chance for rebirth. While he waits, we continue with our partnership.

I have an appointment with the Governing Board to discuss the problems that plagued our case. Heads might roll, though this time, not from Percy's doing, or mine.

Voyeuse: Trapped!

Her day name is Lisa Verdi. She comes from Ecuador, she's a bit kinky, and she is descended from the Incas, by whom she is empowered. She can sense crimes before they are committed, and the sensation arouses her—so she watches, to intervene at the very last moment, because she's the one she pleases.

Now one of the two people she cares most about has been taken prisoner by the ghost of Pizarro, the Spanish conquistador who destroyed the Inca Empire and murdered Lisa's Inca ancestor. Pizarro now wants to kill Voyeuse. Lisa can't go to the police, who have orders to arrest her. Her only hope is to negotiate an exchange—one that will surely result in her death.

So what's a superheroine to do? One thing at a time...

https://www.hiraethsffh.com/product-page/voyuese-trapped-by-tyree-campbell

The Great Harmonic Convergence
John Stratton

"So, Michael, are you going to listen to me?"

"It's not that I'm not listening."

"You have to keep your thoughts bouncing around like a butterfly. You can't let them stick. If you're too tense or stuck on one idea, the process just won't work. Keep your thoughts light and airy, like a butterfly."

"I'm trying, Billy. I really am. It's not that I'm not trying."

"Oh, I know. I know." He waved his hands in front of him and straddled the wicker chair. "Hell, you're better than I am right now. Your sister is right, you've got a real talent for this." He took a long draw on his cigarette and put it in the ashtray on the floor, next to his can of root beer. "But you can appreciate what I'm saying. You can't let your conscious thoughts get in the way of a psychic message. You shouldn't even be thinking in sentences.

"Now you take me, for instance. I haven't had a complete thought in my head since Agnes and I got into this business. Don't even want one. I'm more receptive that way to undercurrents and things of that nature. But you, you're too tense. That's what your headaches are all about."

"They're not migraines."

"I know they're not migraines, but they hurt, don't they? And the left side, that's your psychic side. That's the side you're fighting. That's the side you need to develop. So, are you going to listen to me?

"I'm listening, Billy, but I don't think I have the personality for this kind of thing."

"What kind of personality are you supposed to have? I've watched you do practice readings for Agnes. You're great. But listen, Michael, there are two things you must never do. Never ask a question. Always tell the client, never ask. Don't say 'has your father passed on?' Say 'your father has passed on, hasn't he?' If you're wrong, you'll find out. And secondly, never bring up the bad character traits of the person sitting in front of you, even if you see it loud and clear. That's called letting in negative energy. It also makes the client mad." He picked up his cigarette and drew on it again. "Once you get this down right, you'll be charging as much as I do -- sixty, maybe eighty dollars an hour. A couple of months of that would get you through medical school, wouldn't it?"

"It sure would, if I don't fail this semester."

"Well, if you did, it would be the best thing that could happen to you. Then you could do readings full time and make twice the money you would have made as a doctor. And you do have the gift. You really do, Michael. Both Agnes and I see it in you. And there's a demand for it these days. You don't have to be good. You don't even have to be right half the time. You just have to be there. Do you see what I'm saying?"

I breathed out a long, agonized sigh and clutched my head with both hands. "How many more of these sessions do we have?"

"One. Then you graduate." He opened his large, black scheduling book. "One more appointment with you, one more reading for your sister, then I go off in August for the Great Harmonic Convergence."

"The what?"

"The harmonic convergence. Most important week of the year, most important week of the ages. All the energy in the universe converges on one tree in the Midwest. I'm going to be there when it happens." He reached inside his shirt pocket and threw a photograph across the table. "Look, there I am at the pre-celebration we had last year. Pretty sharp, heh?"

I picked up the picture of Billy dressed in overalls and a country straw hat, with a banjo at his side. Next to him, three other men were dressed the same, each with a different guitar, zither or homemade instrument. They stood behind a sign that read 'Billy Murtree and the Appalachian Mountaineers.'

"I've got one of these already, Billy. You gave it to me

six months ago."

"Well, I'll have new ones for you soon." He tucked the picture back in his pocket. "Hell, I'm just an old mountain boy, Michael. All I know is blue grass music and telling fortunes, but I'm pretty good at both of them. What I really miss are summer nights in the Foothills, where you could tell a folk tale in the hollers and listen to coyotes baying at the moon." He ran his hand through his stark white hair. "Changed the color of my hair once, I can tell you that, when a haint came running after me."

"Why'd you ever leave the Foothills, Billy?"

"Had to. Telling a ghost story was one thing, bringing back your dead mother-in-law was another. Some folks figured talking to the dead was crossing a line. They run me out of town."

"Oh." I looked into the distance as if I could hear coyotes howling.

"Did Agnes tell you we're thinking of opening up a healing center?"

"Yeah, she did."

"You should come with us, you know. You'd be good, Michael. You're better than I am right now."

The screen door slammed in the distance and a small woman carrying groceries waved to us from the kitchen. A long, silver braid hung over her shoulder and seemed to dance across her denim blouse.

"There's Agnes now." He looked at his watch. "Your time's about up anyway, Mike. Remember what I said. Practice with people. Just rattle off the top of your head what you see about them. It'll come."

I slid off my chair and straggled out to the kitchen porch, with Billy's hand at my back, pushing me along.

Agnes smiled at me as I made my way outside. "Aren't you staying for dinner, Michael?"

"No ma'am, thank you anyway. I have a lot of studying to do."

"But it's summer."

"Michael studies all year, don't you Mike?"

I nodded. They both agreed I looked tired and stared at me the way doctors sometimes do when they make a mental diagnosis. I felt miserable all over; tired and cranky and deeply ungrateful for what these two were trying to do for me. But that's not what I told them.

"Look, Billy, I can't thank you enough for what you're doing, teaching me the trade the way you are, and it's not that I'm not grateful, it's just that, I don't know if I'm cut out for this."

"You mean you don't know if you believe in it."

I opened my mouth to protest, but he held up his hand.

"It's all right, Mike. Belief comes with time."

I smiled and took in the whole picture of him – the red and black plaid shirt bulging over a slight paunch, the open collar revealing a set of tarnished dog tags from active duty, and most of all, that lined and weathered face of an Appalachian Mountaineer without his banjo. We gave each other a big hug and I hugged Agnes too and they waved goodbye to me from their white, wooden porch, like a couple of parents.

I liked those two. I liked being with them, being hugged by them. But I hated leaving by the front door of their house. The neighbors sat on their porches and stared at me as I walked away. They knew what Billy and Agnes were up to. They didn't want psychics in the neighborhood and they didn't want anyone who did business with them. If they had known I was training to be one, they probably would have just about shot me. One scruffy-looking backwoodsman who lived next door used to rock back and forth with a rifle across his lap and stare me down until I was out of sight. I could never wait to get out of that neighborhood.

But the long walks cross-town in the late afternoon were a respite for me. I liked to breathe in the honeysuckle and jump down the craggy path through the evergreen forest just outside the city limits. The sun would shimmer over the trees, sending red light into their branches, and I felt good inside, as if I belonged to that forest with the red sun and the chattering crickets. It was all a part of Agnes and Billy.

When I reached my dark apartment, the message light

on the house phone was blinking. It was my sister's voice.

"Mike, it's Isabel. Give me a call. I just want to know how Dr. McAllister is doing with his psychic lessons."

Dr. McAllister. Would I ever be Dr. McAllister?

I opened the refrigerator door to reach for a pot of burned oatmeal. With a brown, wooden ladle, I started stirring the mush over a low flame. It looked like an animal's brains, the kind we would throw away at the lab. Pinned to the corkboard above the stove was the picture of Billy and his mountain band smiling over their banjos. Most of my friends didn't understand that picture. My father, a doctor himself, pulled it off the wall one day and asked, 'Is this why you're failing medical school?'

It was hard to explain Billy away. You didn't just tell people he was a psychic healer who was training you for a part-time job during medical school. You certainly didn't tell that to a retired doctor who was expecting you to take over a practice he had spent a lifetime building up.

Stirring the oatmeal harder, I watched it stick to the sides of the pot and sizzle. "Gypsies," I mused out loud over the flames. "Couple of rootless gypsies, both of them. If I had any sense, I'd get away from them."

But sense was getting harder to hold onto as school bills mounted. I had already failed anatomy because I was carrying two jobs plus a full course load, and most jobs paid minimum wage. Here was a chance to make sixty an hour, just as Billy promised, with more study time in the bargain. How could I say no to that?

I picked up the kitchen wall phone, dialed Isabel and waited to hear her voice. Whenever I did, it was like we were kids again. When she got on the line this time, she sounded exuberant.

"Michael, how's it going? Billy tells me you have one more lesson left before you can take on clients. Aren't you excited?"

"Yeah, I really am."

"Didn't I tell you that you have a gift for this? Billy says you're the most gifted psychic he's ever trained."

I leaned my ear against the receiver. "It's intuition, Isabel."

"Oh, now there you go again. You still don't believe and you know how that hurts me. Honestly, you're the one with the gift. Don't you see how important this is?"

She had a pout to her voice that told me I had ruined the whole party. Then she said, "I know you think I'm crazy, but Agnes and Billy are the only two people who have put me in touch with Arthur. They really have, Mike."

Silence.

"Well, I know you think I'm crazy."

"No, Isabel. I never said you were crazy. I never said that about you at all."

"Well, I know you think so." Her voice drooped. She was starting to cry. I could see her crying right through the phone; her make-up running, and all that red hair wilting around her face. It would tear your heart out to see Isabel cry, and I had a real knack for making it happen. She was sobbing about Arthur now, about how they had had five beautiful years together before he died, and how she had found him again through Billy and Agnes.

"It's just that I've been so happy lately," she went on, "and I wanted you to be happy with me. But you're not. You don't believe in any of this and you think I'm crazy."

It was awful listening to her. I couldn't get a word in, and when I did, it was wrong.

Finally, after a few minutes of silence, she said "Mike, are you there?"

"Yeah, I'm still here." I cleared my throat. "Look, Isabel, I'm sorry. I wouldn't hurt you for the world, you know that. You'll just have to be patient with me. What do you expect from a guy who's spent the last year cutting up pigs?"

She laughed. It was good to hear her laugh. She forgave me. I could tell.

Finally, she said "Mike, are you taking care of yourself? Are you eating all right?"

"Absolutely. In fact, I'm heating up some oatmeal right now."

She winced. "You'll have to do better than that. If you're going to do readings, you'll have to build up your energy. It takes a lot of energy, you know."

"Yeah, I've been told that." I glanced at the picture of the Mountaineer Band. "Hey, Billy tells me you've got a reading coming up before he goes away. What are you going to ask him?"

"You know what I'm going to ask him. I'm going to ask him if I can talk to Arthur."

We laughed.

"Okay pal, put in a good word for me."

"You know I will. Just do everything Billy tells you."

I hung up the receiver and knocked the whole phone set off the wall. "This thing has to go," I murmured. "A decent tin can with a wire would do a better job."

Coaxing globs of burnt oatmeal into a bowl, I watched the phone guts still dangling above the coffee maker. "Readings. Whoever heard of a reading, anyway? In thirty years of life, I've never heard of a reading until I came across Billy and Agnes." I looked back at the band photo. "People who take advantage of grief, they ought to be shot."

Walking over to the kitchen table, I stopped in front of a cabinet mirror and watched myself eat. "Michael, you are too thin. Sunken eyes. Hollow cheeks. When was the last time you cut your hair?" I brushed it out of my eyes. It was the color Isabel's used to be. "At this rate you won't live to graduate from any school." I stared down at the oatmeal. "Your sister's right. You'll have to do better than that."

I went into my room to stretch out on the bed. On the night table was a photo of Isabel and Arthur when they were first married. She looked more like me then. She really did.

People who take advantage of grief, they ought to be shot.

And yet, there had been such a change in Isabel. Phony or real, the sessions with Billy had given her something I didn't want to take away. She was happier, more at peace, better than I had seen her the whole two years since Arthur's death. After he died, she didn't want to do anything. She wouldn't leave the house. When she found Agnes and Billy, all that changed. Billy told her

Arthur was still with her, right by her side, and he loved her. He told her things only Arthur would know, about snow in the mountains when they were building their first house, and a bird's nest they saved from a blizzard. She perked up and seemed to want to live again. She never cried much after that except when I would get on my soap box about both of them being fakes. So, I stopped.

After all, I listened to their readings too. Agnes told me about former lives I had lived, how I had been a doctor in a previous life and I would be one again. I would make it. It would just take time.

Then Isabel reminded me about my own psychic gifts, how I could predict things and they'd come true, or look at people and tell everything about them and I'd be right. I'd had this ability since childhood and used it to entertain friends. I called it intuition, but Billy looked at me and said I had three spirit guides hovering near me and for thirty bucks a throw, he'd teach me how to use them to be a psychic reader, or even a trance medium. Isabel jumped all over that and for sixty dollars an hour, I'd do almost anything except become a male prostitute. Then I started to worry that I was being a prostitute after all.

I put my wooden ladle down and turned Isabel's picture away. I wasn't hungry. I walked over to the window and breathed in the mid-summer air. In the courtyard below, a woman was playing with her dog. I wanted to be out in the woods again, the ones leading up to Billy's house. Instead, I felt chained to the heavy anatomy books lying on the bed, obliged to open them up and read the passages I had failed last year. So I sat down again and scanned pages of meaningless words with summer eyes that didn't care to read anything. I thought about my next session with Billy, just beyond the red forest full of evergreens. And I fell asleep.

My final session with Billy was a lot of mental gymnastics. We practiced telepathy, immediate impressions, and searching out hidden objects, which Billy said was hard to do. I was exhausted after an hour, but relieved that I didn't have my one-sided headache. Billy said that was good. That was because I wasn't fighting my psychic abilities anymore.

Then he got out his cigarettes and his ashtray and his can of soda and straddled the seat of his chair again. "You're good, Mike. You're really good. You're ready to do readings."

"Great." I felt like a prize fighter trained for the ring. I felt like prancing and sparring.

"Now I'm just going to give you a rundown on some general things. If you're going to do readings even part of the time, there are some standards you have to follow. You probably know what they are. No intoxicants of any kind. No drugs, no booze. No promiscuity whatever. Don't hate or hold any kind of anger or jealousy toward anyone. While you're doing readings, eat plenty of high-calorie foods. Lots of orange juice between sessions. You're going to need all the energy you can get. You're a conductor, see?"

I got quiet and put my head down on my arms. "Are you serious, Billy?"

"Never more serious in my life."

"You live like that? I mean, I've heard you and Agnes fight. I've heard you say awful things about people. You keep a standard that strict?"

"No, I don't always live up to it. But the more I do, the better it works. You'll see, once you get started."

I blinked and gazed out the window. "Do you see entities? I mean, you really see people standing there?"

"Yes, I can see entities."

"I've never seen an entity in my life, or an aura, or any of those things you talk about."

"That's okay. You will in time. Sometimes it helps if you turn the lights down. Then you can see a lot in the room."

I got a chill, as if he were telling folk tales again.

"Of course," he smiled, "if you're afraid, it probably won't happen." He took a sip from his stale soda and put it down on the floor again. "You've got a lot of fear in you, Mike. More than you know. You'll want to watch that. Fear pulls in more fear. It pulls in consequences. If there is any single piece of advice I would give you, it's to get rid of fear. In this business you can't afford to have it."

"I'll do my best, Billy."

"Oh, you'll do fine." He started winding his pocket watch. "Well, that's it, Mike. You've graduated. There isn't another thing I can teach you. I've taught you everything I know."

I glanced around the room at the shelves cluttered with tea cups and angel statues, the flowered wallpaper with stripes through the roses, and all of it seemed to say to me 'you're one of us now. You're a psychic.' I wasn't sure I wanted to be one. I put my head back down on my arms.

"Agnes and I will be packing tonight," Billy said. "Next week we'll be heading out for the Midwest to observe harmonic energy converging on one tree. Remember?"

"Is it time already?"

"Just about. The band will be joining us too, bringing their instruments along. Only the bass fiddle has to be sent ahead because it doesn't fit in the back of the van."

"Enjoy yourself, Billy."

"Thanks. I have one more reading with Isabel, then we're ready to go. It'll be good to see her again."

"She thinks a lot of you and Agnes."

"She's been doing much better since I put her in touch with Arthur."

Exploiting grief. I didn't like that.

"I'd ask you to come with us but I have better plans for you. While we're gone, I want you to take on our clients."

I lifted my head. "What?"

"Our clients. I want you to do readings for them while we're gone."

"Me?" I stabbed at my chest with my finger.

"Of course, you. I've got a full caseload, Mike. The whole week is booked and I can't just let these people down. A lot of them have been waiting for months and they're coming hundreds of miles." He showed me the open pages of his appointment book, each square crammed full of names and dates written in a tiny, crimped hand. "I want you to take them. It will be good for you and for them. I want you to meet them. You're a psychic now."

"Billy, I can't do this."

"Why not? It'll mean money, Mike. If you stick to the caseload, I figure, oh," he reached for his calculator and punched a few buttons, "at least fifteen hundred a week, not including weekends."

"Fifteen hundred," I murmured. "But, don't you have any files on these people or anything? Some information I can use as a back-up?"

"This isn't a doctor's office, Mike. We don't keep files on people here. And," he smiled, "it's not the racket you think it is, either."

"Oh, I'm not saying it's a racket, Billy. I haven't said that at all."

"Just rattle off the top of your head. You've never been wrong yet. Keep the butterfly moving like I told you. Remember the bouncing butterfly thoughts?"

"Oh, that." I scratched my forehead as if that butterfly were gnawing right into my brain. "I don't know, Billy. I don't know about this one." The left side of my head started to pound.

But there was no arguing with Billy, or Agnes for that matter. Starting Monday, I was to do readings. The only favor Billy asked was that I do them at their house, where his clients were most comfortable, and that I do them in the kitchen with the green lamp turned low. That's what their clients expected. That's how it was best to do readings, with the lamp turned low. I could have my fill of the refrigerator and even sleep in their guest room if I wanted. They really were generous, both of them. And when they gave me their key and packed me off that night, I felt as if I had graduated from medical school instead of shamanism.

When Monday came, I decided not to sleep at Billy's house. I attended classes until two in the afternoon, studied at the library for three hours, and started toward the outskirts of the city around five. By the time I reached the quiet neighborhood of white framed houses, it was five-thirty. People were sitting on their porches, watching me walk up the path. They knew the Murtrees weren't home. On the porch next door, the backwoodsman sat forward over his rifle to stare at every move I made. When I stared back, I looked into the face of the toughest, roughest-looking cuss I'd ever laid eyes on. He had a stubbly, half-grown beard and wore overalls I could almost smell from across the lawn. He had his nerve sitting forward like that, clutching his rifle while I picked up the mail and fumbled with the house key. I could feel his eyes on me the whole time I tried to get the front door open. So much for him. Soon clients would be showing up, parking their cars outside and there would be plenty of action for these clowns to watch.

I followed Billy's advice and poured a glass of orange juice from the refrigerator. Then I put the glass and the pitcher on the kitchen table next to the lamp with the green shade. I turned up the lamp and pulled down the shades against brilliant sunlight streaking across the table. I unlatched the back kitchen door, sat down in front of Billy's appointment book and checked my schedule. My first client was at six o'clock. It was six now.

When I heard the parlor door open, I walked into the living room to introduce myself, explaining who I was and why Billy wasn't there. A stout, middle-aged woman, Emma Shepherd didn't even seem disappointed. She followed me into the kitchen and sat down at the table in the green circle of light.

I cleared my throat. "Is your husband dead, Mrs. Shepherd?"

Rule number one broken. Never ask a question.

"Yes, he is."

"I would say he's been dead some six months now."

"That's right. Five and a half months almost to the day."

"I sense his presence very strongly. He's with us, you know."

She pulled out a handkerchief and started to cry. "I know. I sense it too."

I got the impression this woman was cheating with money. 'Don't break rule number two,' I said to myself. 'Don't bring up negative character traits.' I let her cry for a while.

Then I said, "Mrs. Shepherd, are you having financial troubles?"

Her tears stopped abruptly. "Why do you ask?"

Touchy ground. Back off. Focus on his name.

"I'm getting an H-A-R. Your husband's name was Harvey or Harold."

"Harmon."

"Harmon wants me to tell you something." I struggled for a minute to clean up the message. "He wants me to tell you to stop writing checks from your daughter's trust fund."

She dropped her handkerchief and stared at me with her mouth open. You can bet old Billy never said anything like that to her.

You really did it this time. Probably lost your first client.

But oddly enough she sat quietly and told me she was in debt from her husband's funeral.

I told her that her husband was going to provide a way for her. Harmon was still looking out for her welfare. I sensed it.

The reading turned pleasant. I settled back. This woman hugged me. And she paid me.

The next client came in. I could hear the parlor door open and close several times. People were filling up the waiting room now, talking. Some were surprised to see me. Others not so much. I sipped orange juice between sessions. I was very accurate. Everybody liked me. I got better as the night wore on.

Soon the kitchen grew black and the circle of light brighter, greener. Soon the orange juice pitcher was half full, then empty. I was tired but content. The kitchen table drawer was getting filled with cash, ten and twenty-dollar bills. It made me uneasy, all that cash. I shrugged it off.

The parlor got quiet. I stood up to stretch, thinking it was well past midnight and time to lock up. I picked up the appointment book to start looking at the next day's names, checking off who I had seen that night. Someone had walked into the room and was standing in the corner.

"You can come in," I motioned without looking up.

"Just have a seat and I'll be with you."

No one moved. I looked up. It was Arthur. There was no mistake about it. I would know that face and moustache anywhere. It was Arthur standing in the corner of the room.

"Oh my God," I staggered backward and slammed into the edge of the table, dropping the book and knocking the lamp to the floor, its green plastic shade rolling against the sink. The table slid from under me and I fell against the wall. When I looked up, no one was there.

I shook uncontrollably as I reached for the lamp, then slumped back against the wall and covered my face with my hands. Billy had set me up for this, talking about dimmed rooms and entities and Arthur. Not only had I seen my brother-in-law as real as life, but I had heard him in my head. He had held out his hand and said 'don't worry, I'm here to protect you.'

Now if there's one thing I can't stand hearing from anyone, living or dead, it's 'don't worry, I'm hear to protect you.' It scared me. The whole thing scared me. I got up and righted the lamp shade. I straightened the table and sat down, trying to catch my breath.

It was time to get out of this racket. I didn't care if it was real. I didn't care if it was imagined. I didn't even care about the fifteen hundred dollars anymore. I just wanted out.

I was getting ready to leave, collecting the cash from the middle drawer of the table, when someone else came into the room, someone alive this time, I was certain. He pulled the chair out of the circle of light and sat down. I could hear his breathing but couldn't see his face, he was so far out of the light.

"Just give me a minute," I said, "I'll be right with you."

"Are you Billy Murtree?" The voice asked.

"No, I'm sitting in for him."

"Where's Billy Murtree?"

"He went out west somewhere for a religious celebration."

"Are you in this with him?"

"What?" I strained to see the man's face.

"You and Billy Murtree. are you in this together?"

"Do I have an appointment with you?" I looked down my list of names. The last appointment ended at eleven o'clock. This man was not scheduled. "Who are you, anyway?"

"You're the psychic. You tell me."

Something coiled inside of me.

He sat forward. I could see his nose and mouth, but not his eyes.

"I want to know how Billy knew about the body."

"What?"

His chair creaked as he leaned even closer. Still his eyes were in blackness. "Look, you don't think for one minute I buy this psychic act. If Billy knew where that girl's body was, he was there and saw who did it. Did he say who did it?"

"I don't know what you're talking about. Get out of here."

"Get out, hell."

I heard a click and caught sight of the barrel of a snub-nosed pistol trained on me.

"Who *are* you?"

"Just tell me if Billy saw who killed that girl, or if you did. You might as well come clean with me, because you're not getting out of here alive. Nobody's left in that waiting room. Nobody's left in the whole house. So don't waste my time."

I heard the trigger click a second notch. Then the sound of gunshot peppered the walls and I shut my eyes, certain that I was hit. But I wasn't. There was no sting, just the endless ricochet of that single shot. I opened my eyes. My attacker lay sprawled across the floor, clutching his wrist. Next to my foot, his gun lay open with the cartridge blown in half. I leaned over to pick it up.

"No, no, fella. Don't touch that pistol. It's evidence."

A voice at the screen door made me jump and turn around. It was the man from next door, the backwoodsman whose stubble-bearded face I had never wanted to see again. He leaned his smoking rifle against the wall and turned on the switch to the top light. Another man in overalls brushed past him and bent over the writhing figure, fitting handcuffs to his wrists.

My neighbor stood in front of me with his hands on his belt and smiled. "Are you okay?"

"I think so." I ran my hand over my head. "How did you ever know what was going on in here from your porch?"

"I wasn't on my porch. I was on yours." He pointed to the screen door with his thumb, as if he were hitchhiking. "Right out there, on the steps outside the kitchen. I've been sitting there since six o'clock." He reached into the pocket of his overalls and flipped open a wallet to show a badge. "I'm a federal undercover agent. Understand now?"

I shook my head. "No, I don't understand at all."

In the corner, his partner was ankle-cuffing my would-be murderer, talking with muted tones into a spitting police radio.

"Didn't Billy tell you we were staking the place out?"

"Billy told me nothing. What's going on?"

"I brought him into a murder case back in February, to see if he could psych out where the body was. And he was right on target. He gave us the exact spot on an abandoned farm by a creek, just across the state line. Even gave us the numbers off the fencepost. And there she was." He took out a cigarette and offered one to me.

"Wait a minute, let me get this straight. You called Billy Murtree from an FBI building and used his services as a psychic to help you solve a murder?"

"That's right. I've known Billy for years and he's always willing to help."

"And you believe in this stuff?"

He hunched his shoulders. "No, not exactly. But when you're desperate, well, you take help in any form it's offered."

He held his lighter up to my cigarette, but my hand shook so badly I couldn't keep it still.

"Here, let me do that for you." He got my cigarette started and handed it back to me. "Trouble was, Billy's name and hometown address wound up on a national wire service. So, he got afraid that the murderer would come back here and try to kill him. And he was right again."

"Well, that's only common sense."

"Sure, that's only common sense. So, I told Billy I'd stake him out myself as a personal favor."

I shuddered as if a wind had chilled the room. "I'm glad you were there."

"Me too," he smiled. "You know, for a while there, watching you come and go from here all those months, I wasn't sure the murderer wasn't you." He smiled a grin that took up his whole dirty face. "Why don't you give me your name and phone number?"

"Oh, do I have to? I mean, I'd as soon nobody knew I was here, involved in this. Does my name have to go on record, or something?"

"I don't see why. But I'd like to have it anyway. You never know. Someday I might be asking you where the bodies are buried."

And with that, he slapped me on the back and laughed out loud. I heard sirens in the distance. My first night as a psychic was over.

When Agnes and Billy came home, I turned all of their clients over to them. They both said how grateful they were that I had been there, how fortunate it was that the murder was solved, but how sorry they were that it all had converged on me. Billy gave me another picture of himself, this time standing on a mountain top with his hands stretched out to the sky. Agnes brought back a carved wooden horse for me and a zither harp.

On August 25th I walked out of Billy Murtree's world and went back to cutting up pigs. I never did hear from him again. I never gave another reading. I got a job in a garage and never went near the white houses on the other side of the evergreen forest. It shook me up that Billy worked on murder cases. It rattled me that he knew where even one body was even once in his whole lifetime. And above all, it terrified me that I had seen Arthur for the space of even one second in the kitchen of a house I didn't own.

Isabel wouldn't talk to me after I left Agnes and Billy. It was months before she forgave me for turning my back on my gift. I never did tell her what I saw in that darkened room on the night I was nearly killed. But I never forgot it. To this day, when August rolls around and the crickets chatter outside, I think about Billy's kitchen and I glance into the corners of the room, hoping to reassure myself that phantoms don't exist.

It's the price I've paid for being a prostitute.

Tidings of Madness and Joy
The ABCs of the Great Old Ones

Greetings, Mortal! In these pages you will find tales of madness, see things beyond imagining, and you - yes YOU! - can bring them to life. Do you dare learn more about the Great Old Ones? Will you give them that which they crave? Or will you find yourself screaming as you learn absolute truth and see through the Great Beyond. Only time will tell. Come along and see what the Great Old Ones have to offer...

This is an incredibly unique coloring book and we are thrilled to finally be able to release it.

Get more dark and twisted tales with it and enjoy bringing the Old Gods to life in various ways.

https://www.hiraethsffh.com/product-page/tidings-of-madness-and-joy-by-marcia-borell-bill-otto

Grinning Death
Scott Coutourier

In majestic pageantry the Grinning Death does go –
'round & 'round in ravenous route to overthrow
all that we have built, all we create & know.

Called up truly from Time's unruly tomb,
offspring of Nature's ruddy & weeping womb,
come solely to ravage & rampage – to consume.

All our world struck like a leper's bell
as Grinning Death grimly gnashes its knell,
throat bottomless, an ever-hungry well.

Oceans recede to alkaline seepage:
clouds retreat to horizons of another age
as graves gape wearily to receive their wage –

In pageantry's wake comes a pale shroud
to lay over brow of a race once-proud,
quiet where before was wailing loud.

The Parapsychologist
Roger Lime

John Tackett was lightheaded and felt like he needed to throw up. His stomach churned as he tossed and turned on the doctor's felt-tufted chaise lounge.

A dense dreary spray of rain pattered loudly against the window of the second-floor brownstone office where Tackett sat. Outside, the east end of the city thoroughfare, normally congested with buzzing cars, rambling homeless, and foulmouthed pedestrians, was deathly vacant.

Everything inside the office was excessive and confounding. The office smelt overpoweringly of cypress bark potpourri, lemon incense, and old man musk. Tackett was surrounded by walls of foreign literature stored on rickety shelving and powdery tan wallpaper printed with an infinite swarm of dragonflies. The insect-ridden wallpaper was, to Mr. Tackett, a dizzying and profoundly uncomfortable design choice.

On the wall behind a wide mahogany pedestal desk was a nigh endless series of convoluted degrees and accreditations: a Bachelor of Arts in Egyptology and Assyriology from Brown University; a Doctor of Medicine from the University of Pittsburgh; a psychiatric residency and psychical research certification from the Division of Perceptual Studies at the University of Virginia School of Medicine's Department of Psychiatry & Neurobehavioral Sciences; graduate certificates in thanatology from Hood College and in astrobiology from the University of Washington.

The man who sat across from Tackett was an odd sort. He was a bespectacled hairless man--ambiguously mixed-race and aged somewhere between forty and eighty--dressed in a mismatched, ill-fitted thrift suit. He was a looming figure whose twisting, towering form crouched awkwardly in his chair in order to situate himself. In spite of his long build, the man was emaciated and could not have weighed any more than one hundred and sixty pounds. Protruding from his disproportionately large head was a Brobdingnagian snout which hooked out like Gonzo the Great's, and the loose, spoilt flesh that hung off his bones glistened with moisture which made his face look like a sallow papier-mâché mask. He had on the severe expression of an austere cardinal or a goose-stepping fascist and his eyes were glowing grey orbs which cut through his cloudy goggles like blazing beams of dead light javelining through seaboard fog.

The Office of Dr. Virgil S. Leeds, Parapsychologist, Tackett had read in a published review. *We all have our personal demons. But you don't have to live with them anymore. Through its unique direct action approach, the revolutionary technique of Dr. Leeds eclipses all mainstream psychotherapies. Go visit the practice of Dr. Leeds on 41 Emerald Ave. to uncover, confront, and slay your demons once and for all.*

The entirety of Tackett's time in the doctor's office had been characterized by non-stop bizarro interactions. Even from their very first greeting, Tackett had been taken aback by the doctor's handshake. While maintaining unbroken eye contact, the doctor had initially taken Tackett's hand in an ordinary handshake. However, as the two men started to let loose from the handshake, the doctor suddenly gripped Tackett's hand and brushed the side of his hand with each finger, one-by-one, before pushing his hand up and off. So peculiar was the maneuver that Tackett found himself absentmindedly computing the handshake throughout the entire introduction of the session. Was it some oddball flirtation? A meaningless hand spasm?

"Tell me about Matthew," ordered the doctor. His voice rasped out from between his gritted teeth like an industrial hiss. The doctor seemed to be more of an inquisitor than psychotherapist. He did not invite voluntary confessionals, but rather he silently extracted them in an invisible, mechanical autopsy with cold, sterilized tools. Tackett felt prosecuted, and so he looked down and avoided eye contact as he confided his tragedy to Dr. Virgil Leeds.

"My son," began Mr. Tackett, "was born with Patau

syndrome. Doctors call it Trisomy 13 because it results from the total duplication of the thirteenth chromosome. This comes with more genetic abnormalities than can be counted. Cognitive developmental disorders, bilateral anophthalmia, microcephaly, polydactyly, cleft palate--to name just a few. He can't see or hear. And he is severely disfigured."

"I love my son. I want to love my son. But every time I look at him, I become filled with dread. He makes me sick. I don't even see him as human. He's so hideously mangled. My boy--my sweet baby boy--is a subhuman creature to me. A human child has an upper lip, a nose, five-fingered hands. Matthew has none of these things. Oh God, he is so horribly ruined. I don't know how this could have happened. Casandra and I are so healthy. We have no glaring family histories of inheritable genetic mutations. The doctors say it just happened. The haphazard, ruined, discarded art project of an unartful, uncaring god. He shouldn't exist at all; not the way he does. His birth was cruelty itself. I don't know what to do. I don't know how I can be a father to him when I can't even look at him."

"I feel guilty and horrible. How could a dad say such things and think such thoughts about his own child? I am disgusted by my own son. But I'm even more disgusted by myself."

"At night, I lie in bed beside my wife. I hear Matthew cry from down the hall. He cries like a normal baby boy. He sounds so scared and alone. In those moments, when I can hear him but not see him,--those are the only moments when he feels like my son. My true son. I imagine him in a better world. He's complete, healthy, and beautiful. Perfectly human. In this better world, I can love him as wholly as a father should love his son. I want to escape to this world. I want to go and be with my son. But I can't go to him. I can't be there to comfort him. I know as soon as I see him that the fantasy will shatter, and he'll just be this deformed, writhing monster again. And so I just lie in bed, crying and choking at the ceiling. I pretend to be asleep, waiting until my wife will finally get up and go rock Matthew to sleep herself. She sees past the ugliness and sees the precious miracle hidden beneath the folds of twisted skin. She's such a good mother. And I am such a wretched father."

Tackett's chin curled into his gullet, and he gulped out a sob. Dr. Leeds became a blur as Tackett's eyes filled with tears. "I'm helpless. Pathetic. What kind of father would leave his child alone like that? What kind of repulsive coward is too afraid of his baby boy to comfort him when he is afraid? What kind of home is that for an infant, where his own father can't stomach the sight of him?"

"There are times when I think about killing him to put him out of his misery--and me out of mine. And then I resurface, and I want to kill myself for thinking such an evil thing."

As Tackett wept, Dr. Leeds made no attempt to comfort or console him or even to offer him a tissue. He simply stared at him as though he were a specimen exhibited in a Plexiglas terrarium for his observation.

"What have you heard about my services, Mr. Tackett?" Dr. Leeds asked, breaking the monotony of his patient's sobs.

Wiping his eyes and nose with his shirt, Tackett replied, "I've heard that you can get inside people's heads and confront their personal demons. Non-figuratively speaking."

"Hmm. More or less. Do you believe in ghosts, John?"

"I don't know. I guess I believe that there are certain things that cannot be easily explained by science."

"That is a lazy and disingenuous answer. Insipid, sheepish idiots are programmed by their pathetic inhibitions to recite that worthless answer in lieu of actually exploring the question. And so I ask again. Do you believe in ghosts, John? Yes or no. Do not equivocate with me."

"No," said John, leery of an impending quack monologue, "Do you?"

"No I don't--at least not in the traditional understanding of ghosts in folklore. I do, however, believe that real preternatural phenomena is merely an extension of psychology. I believe in collective memory and trauma, of which ghosts--or more accurately *tulpas* are manifestations," said Dr. Leeds, "My technique utilizes this interpretation of ghosts. There are four components of the treatment I use: the *domain*, the *tulpa*, the *trauma*, and you."

"I believe that the human psyche, or consciousness, is in and of itself a dimension which is indirectly accessible to outside individuals. I refer to this dimension in my work as the *domain*. In the context of this treatment, the domain is a setting conjured by your consciousness, founded loosely both upon a central place of memory as well as the empty, malleable void of your subconscious imagination. I believe that certain complex forms of transpersonal communication operate as revolving-door portals into and out of the domain. Consequently, things can enter the domain--most typically, experiences which in turn convert to memories--and, very rarely, things can exit."

"Tulpas are the psychical incarnations of memories, perceptions, and traumas. Moreover, they are a certain subtype of parapsychological phenomena that may directly enter and exit the domain. What individuals perceive to be 'ghosts' in haunted places are in reality escaped manifestations from individual domains. When a memory, particularly a trauma, is so overpowering to an individual, it may free itself from its individual's domain and escape into the mortal realm where it may be communicable to others. Hence why most 'haunted' places are sites of past atrocities--the ghosts of these sites are escaped tulpas of the victims' personal internal trauma, rather than reincarnated forms of decedents. Hence why certain tulpas may not resemble anyone at all. They are immortalized figments of events, not exclusively of people."

"My technique involves entering my patient's domain through my patient's dreams, which I have determined to be points of entry and exit, to accompany and guide them to directly confront their trauma. I do not literally enter your mind. Your own perception and short-term memory of me does. My work involves narrowly tailoring your perception of me--my tulpa in the limited context of treatment--so that it operates as I wish within the confines and constructs of your mind. My infiltration is by proxy, through the ephemeral guiding form of my tulpa. The most difficult stage of the technique is empowering the tulpa to escape after the direct confrontation so that we can transfer its observations to me."

"Why does that need to happen?"

"So that I can verify that you've not been deranged by the treatment. The worst thing that can happen is for our direct confrontation with the trauma to make things worse--namely by *feeding* the trauma. In these cases, we need to immediately initiate a subsequent treatment or else you might succumb further to your trauma or even release it into the world as an outward-bound tulpa."

"How do you do access your ghost's observations if it's *my* memory?" Tackett asked, trying to stifle a smirk as he said this ridiculous sounding question out loud.

"A Thelemic variant on transcendental meditation which involves the ingestion of pinyon nuts and salvia divinorum tea."

"Okay. Wow. I'm sorry, this is a lot to take in. It sounds to me half like science fiction and half like Timothy Leary cult nonsense. I don't think I understand any of it at all. Do you have any factual or scientific basis for these theories?" Tackett asked. He also wanted to ask if Dr. Leeds actually went to medical school, but restrained himself.

"You will understand it," assured Dr. Leeds, ignoring Tackett's latter question, "My technique is ineffable. But it is very much demonstrable. I received the completed agreement and liability waiver last week, so your paperwork is in order. Did you follow my instructions before you came over?"

"Yes. I haven't slept in three days. I'm lightheaded and I feel like I need to throw-up."

"Very good," said Dr. Leeds, "Shall we proceed?"

Tackett nodded. Leeds stood up from his chair and went to his desk, fetching something from his drawer. He returned to Tackett and unfurled his clenched, gangly hand, revealing two violet pills in his palm. "Over-the-counter melatonin. They are to be chewed."

"How does this work now? Do you hook me up to a machine like in *Inception*? Or are you supposed to hypnotize me?" asked Tackett.

"There is no such thing as true hypnosis. Only hypnotic situation. Since you first entered my office, I have been gradually placing you in a heightened and compounded state of Transderivational Search within which your perception and memory of me is intensified. This state will enable the hypnotic situation from which you will sink into REM. You will find me--err--my tulpa there."

"In REM?"

"In REM."

Tackett devoured the melatonin pills. Dr. Leeds invited him to laze on the chaise lounge and fall asleep in "whatever position suits you best."

Is this is? Tackett wondered. This is the big, revolutionary *technique*? Did I really pay a thousand dollars for this freak to watch me sleep? Fuck me.

Tackett first laid on his side. As he began to drift off however, this form slowly curled into fetal position. The last thing he saw before he dipped into unconsciousness was Dr. Leeds moving to stand over him. He placed one hand gently on Tackett's pulse. The doctor held something sweet-smelling and smoking in his other hand--but Tackett was too blurredly tired to make it out.

For now, just relax. You are safe here now. Focus on my voice and nothing else. Release all of your stresses, fears, and inhibitions. Detach from the sorrows of reality. Sink away. Flee into fields of fantasy and freedom. Think about your happy place. Go there, and I will find you.

***

Tackett found himself standing vis-à-vis a stout craftsman home in a cul-de-sac in a seemingly endless expanse of white-grass plains.

The sky and grasslands were nothing more than a bland polarity of whitish grey and bluish grey, and all the other homes on the cul-de-sac were just crude oblong blurs. It was as though Tackett had teleported into a landscape painted by a lazy artist who only cared about detailing the single craftsman home in the foreground and nothing else. The craftsman home was a pale-paneled boring thing crowned by three low-pitched triangular roofs and fronted by a modest open porch. It looked like a lot of other houses in a lot of other neighborhoods in a lot of other places. And yet Tackett stared at the house with a look of stark familiarity.

"Whose house is this?" said a voice from behind Tackett. Tackett turned to find Dr. Leeds standing against the infinite plain. He was leaned forwardly against a beechwood dress cane.

"It looks like our house in Leiden Islip from before we moved into the city. Cassandra and I lived here while she was still pregnant with Matthew. Why would we be here though?"

Dr. Leeds pursed his lips and continued looking past Tackett up at the house. "Tell me more about your time in the house."

"We moved here after finishing grad school. Our wedding was in Stowe, but Cass and I were officially married here in a smaller ceremony attended by our immediate families. Matthew was conceived here. We moved into the city shortly before his birth to be closer to Cass's parents so that they could babysit. But this was a wonderful home and we miss living here every day."

"You didn't know Matthew would have Patau syndrome while Cassandra carried him in this home?"

"No. He was diagnosed at St. Leopold's in the city while still in the womb."

"So you were still very hopeful about him while you lived here. Tell me. Did you enjoy placing your hand on your wife's belly and feeling him kick? Did that bring you joy?"

"Yes."

"You loved him. Fully."

"I did."

"Do you hear that?" Dr. Leeds asked Tackett, gesturing

toward the top floor of the house. The patient listened closely. Through the wisping zephyrs of the plains, Tackett could hear the faint sound of crying coming from somewhere inside the house. His son's crying.

And then, a roar. It was a guttural, gargling sound that tremored the house from deep within and even appeared to blow back the long grass outside. It had the erupting power of a lion's roar, but the unstable vibrato of a squealing hog and the wet biological quality of fluids squished in sex. It was an inhuman, extraterrestrial, traumatic noise, one which would haunt its listener's memory for many years to come.

Tackett became pale. "I don't want to go in," he said, turning back to Leeds, "I don't want to be here anymore. I want to wake up. Take me back to your office. The session is over."

Dr. Leeds gazed into Tackett with a look of such violent contempt that it frightened Tackett nearly as much as the roar. "You have been a sniveling coward for the entirety of your short time as a father--and likely long before as well," Dr. Leeds said, "For the first and last time, you have the opportunity to save your infant son from a lifetime of loneliness."

"Fuck you," Tackett said, "You don't know anything about me. You're not even the real Leeds. You're just a figment of my imagination. A ghost."

"To a degree, I'm your conscience."

"Yeah, you're a real Jiminy Cricket." Tackett ran his fingers through his hair and cursed under his breath. "What's even in there, man?" he asked.

"I don't know. Apparently I don't know anything. I'm just a figment of your imagination."

"That--whatever roared. Do you think it can hurt me?"

"Certainly."

"I don't want to go in alone."

"You won't be alone," said Dr. Leeds, taking his cane under his arm, "You're paying me nearly a thousand dollars to go in with you."

With a grimace and a deep breath, Tackett crept up to the front porch of the house. He trekked through freshly-mowed grass and up cobbled stone steps, past the oblong shrubberies, blocky wooden columns, and the white-paneled garage wall--all of which he had not passed in nearly a year. Stopping at the front door, Tackett tried to catch a glimpse inside for a sneak-peek at what awaited him in there, but curtains veiled each and every window. A gangling shadow covered Tackett from behind, like a security blanket tossed over him by a worried mother.

Tackett opened the door.

Like the outside cul-de-sac, the inside of the house was as placid as a still-life. In spite of its apparent vacancy, the home did not feel abandoned or condemned. It was spotlessly maintained and impeccably presentable, like an idyllic nuke town model. The lights were all turned on. There were no shadows. There were no secrets. There was nowhere to hide. To the left was a charming kitchen--uncluttered, unpretentious, and rinsed over by buttery sunlight that poured in from the dining area window. Straight ahead was a living room--inviting and warm.

And to the right was a steep carpeted staircase that climbed up into the blank top floor hallway. Murky footprints were seared into each step, moving upward toward the sound of infantile wails and repetitious battering which echoed stridently from the upstairs hall.

Tackett, followed closely by Dr. Leeds, treaded up the stairs. As he ascended, Tackett's grasp of the rail whitened his knuckles.

Another roar erupted from the upstairs hall, halting Tackett and Leeds in their tracks. Tackett turned to look down at Dr. Leeds, only to find the doctor already staring back at him. "Your mind, your lead," the doctor said.

Tackett arrived upstairs and could finally make out the source of the battering and the roars.

Down the hall, within its claustrophobic chamber of bone-white-painted drywall, a long, sinewy, naked figure cavorted angrily against a single closed door, slapping and scratching at its wood panels with its spidery limbs. Again and again, the monster hurled itself into the door, buckling against the door frame and slashing at it with vengeful ferocity as it braced to lunge again. Because of its height, the monster's scalp and shoulder blades raked the ceiling, taking off the crust and crumbs of decaying paint. Its spine broke through the skin of its back, exposing its jagged vertebrae.

"That," said Dr. Leeds, "Is your trauma."

Suddenly, sensing the visitors' presence, the monster stopped and turned its malformed head toward Tackett and Leeds, exposing to them its biblical hideousness. Its maw was a wet, toothless thing, the top of which extended vertically, running well into the pressed, slab of flesh where its nose should have been--like a gargling river valley splitting through bisected, bulging mounds of folded skin. This mutant valley was buttressed by loose jowls hung lifelessly from under the monster's drooping cheekbones. Its eyes were sunken marbles of gleaming black gore, rolled deep within its cavernous sockets and stretched afar from one another by its plateaued nose bridge.

As a line of viscous drool rolled out of its face, the monster continued to claw at the closed door as it stared at Tackett and Leeds, challenging them to interfere. Behind this door was the source of the cries. Tackett winced at the revelation that, barricaded behind only this splintering door, was a trapped child.

Tackett cried out and clutched his face to blind himself from the horror. And then he turned to leave.

"I don't know who or what is crying in that room," said Dr. Leeds, interrupting Tackett's hasty departure, "But I think you might. And once that trauma gets in, it will almost certainly overwhelm and kill whatever is inside that room. Are you prepared to live with the consequences if that happens?"

Tackett halted, but did not turn. His fists were clenched bone-white and his back was bristled up like an on-guard alley cat. Dr. Leeds waited for his patient to challenge him. He waited for a justification. There was none. The wordless John Tackett proceeded--ostensibly unyielding in his meek cravenness--disappearing past the corner of the hall and moving back downstairs toward the kitchen and exit.

Dr. Leeds sighed. He wiped his glasses. He turned to follow Tackett out and abandon the monster to its violent meal. Perhaps later then, he muttered under his breath. Retreat here and now; muster up for a future charge. We'll be back. A night of self-loathing, a swig of rye, and another installment of $1,000--and we'll be back. No need to time-stamp recovery.

Just as Dr. Leeds neared the end of the hall, Tackett reemerged from the kitchen. In his right hand, Tackett clutched a fire poker. With a look of unwavering resolve, Tackett made his way down the hallway.

The monster hardly had time to react as Tackett plunged the iron implement into the its bony chest. The point landed squarely into the center of the monster's sternum, burrowing deep into its insides.

The monster let out a piercing shriek and whipped its arm out at Tackett, flinging him off. Tackett slammed into the adjacent wall, which fissured from the force of his impact. Tackett fell to the floor and his fire poker fell from his grip some distance away. With a low vindictive snarl, the monster approached Tackett. It crouched to its fallen assailant's height and reached its protracted claw out to the softest part of his neck.

At that moment, Dr. Leeds brought down his walking stick down onto the monster's skull. The metal cane head cracked, caving part of the scalp. The monster jolted forward from the blow, during which Dr. Leeds struck it again--this time in the middle of the spine--, breaking off pieces of vertebrae and felling the monster completely so that, for an auspicious moment, it lay prostrate on the floor. Dr. Leeds struck it again. And again.

During the hammering of the monster by the doctor, Tackett recovered his fire poker from the nearby ground and hastily joined Dr. Leeds's attack, skewering the monster under its ribcage, in its throat, and through its face.

Dr. Leeds continued to bludgeon the monster with the cane as Mr. Tackett continued to stab and disembowel it with the poker. Even when the monster became hopelessly limp, the two men continued to annihilate it. They stabbed and slashed and beat and stomped and slammed its body. Bruised flesh ripped away to bleeding muscle tissue and bleeding muscle tissue ripped away to bone and bone broke away to nothingness. The two men did not stop until they were too exhausted to proceed. By this point, the monster was nothing more than a pulverized mass of splintered bones, torn viscera, and pooling blood. Whereas before it had been disfigured beyond description, now it was disfigured beyond existence.

Dr. Leeds propped against the wall to catch his breath. Tackett, without any semblance of hesitation, took his fire poker to the monster's door like a crowbar, wedged it in, and broke into the locked room.

The space was a sparsely occupied bedroom painted a subdued shade of sky blue. Toys scattered the carpet and, balled up in a cradle, underneath a safari animal mobile, was a crying baby boy. The child writhed on his bed, tangling himself in his plush quilt.

Tackett limped across the bedroom to the cradle, leaving his bloody fire poker behind at the door. He peered down into the cradle at his son. Joshua was eyeless and he had a split lip. He reached up to his father with a six-fingered hand. But aside from these minor deformities, he was still only a human baby boy--nothing like the monster that had stalked him outside his door. He had rosy ears and rosy cheeks. He had a tuft of hay-colored hair that sprouted atop his head. He had little feet that danced in the air with frustration and excitement. Something inexplicable had lifted from John's senses. This was not abject ugliness unlike anything else he had ever witnessed. This was Joshua. And, in light of the preceding horror and for the first time, he was wholly beautiful to his father.

Though he was soaked in blood, sweat, and tears, Tackett reached down and picked up his son. With his arms wrapped tightly around the child, Tackett pressed him to his heaving chest. "I'm sorry," he whimpered hoarsely to his boy, "I'm so sorry. I'm here now. I'm here."

The ghost of Dr. Leeds waited in the archway of the broken door, watching John Tackett pace the room with his son. It was a joy equivalent to that of a father meeting his newborn for the first time. Or, perhaps more accurately, it was that joy precisely.

"I love you, Joshie. Daddy loves you so much."

***

John Tackett awoke on the chaise lounge.

He was drenched in sweat and his shirt was pulled all the way up to his neck. Embarrassed, Tackett quickly pulled it back down and covered his torso, checking to see if he had left behind a sweat mark on the couch. He had.

Dr. Leeds sat in a chair across from him. His eyes were glazed over and his mouth hung open slightly. He looked dead. "Dr. Leeds?" whispered Tackett. Before, the office was soundtracked by the noise of falling rain. But the rain had stopped. Now it was silent.

Tackett nudged Leeds's hand which seemed to resuscitate the old man back to consciousness.

"Is everything alright?" Tackett asked.

"Everything will be fine, John," Dr. Leeds said. He stood up, straightened his jacket, and briefly checked his watch. "Go home now and rest. I will contact you by the end of the week to determine our next steps--if there are any necessary at all."

"Sure. Fine." Tackett said. Despite having just woken up from a long sleep, he felt awkwardly out of breath as he spoke. Mimicking Leeds, Tackett glanced at his own watch. Nine o'clock. Their one-hour session had gone on nearly five hours. "You don't have any paperwork? Or questions for me? Shouldn't we--I don't know--talk about what happened?"

"Not at this time," said Dr. Leeds, "You may leave."

"Oh. Okay. Alright then. Have a good night, doctor."

"You as well, John."

With that, Tackett left.

Once the door closed behind Tackett, Dr. Leeds waited a moment in case the patient came back for something. Then he removed an audio recorder from his inside jacket pocket and hit [stop recording]. Then, from the side table behind the chaise lounge, Dr. Leeds retrieved his yellow legal pad and, with both his notes and recorder, he sat in his chair. Meditation and pinyon nuts, Leeds scoffed. How ridiculous. The first page of his notes, titled *Movements and Visual Observations*, was densely daubed in black blocks of impossibly small hand-jotted scribbles. 00:06:23:87 - John converts to fetal position. 00:07:01:12 - John tightens position. His shirt pulls up, exposing his stomach to the couch fabric. 00:07:09:40 - The contact of the couch on his skin appears to somewhat relax John's muscles. See Harlow. 00:12:56:39 - John appears to have fully entered sleep. 00:13:00:00 - 00:20:00:00 - frequent and fleeting re-awakenings; slow eye movements. Light, non-REM. 00:23:18:41 - John's ring and little fingers on his left hand move rapidly against his belly. Etcetera. Etcetera.

He turned to the second page. *Utterances and Dialogic Observations*. This page was blank. Dr. Leeds opened his pen and pressed [play audio]. *It looks like our house in Leiden Islip from before we moved into the city. Cassandra and I lived here while she was still pregnant with Matthew. Why would we be here though?* Tackett's voice crackled and echoed through the recorder. As the audio played, Dr. Leeds transcribed the content into his journal. He would work well into the night, "conferring with his tulpa."

And somewhere, on the farthest side of the city proper, John Tackett held his son.

Believe nothing you hear, and only one half that you see
– Poe –

Mating Call
Kristi Petersen Schoonover

On Martha's Vineyard, everyone knew the story of Booming Ben, the last living heath hen on the planet.

He was practically a celebrity. Everyone knew he was the lone survivor of the fire that'd taken the rest of his brood. Everyone knew to drive slowly, in case he decided—like some common wild turkey—to run across the road. Everyone knew his sound, like somebody blowing across the top of a beer bottle, and everyone knew he spent each spring calling for a mate that would never come.

Then, on an unusually warm November day, when the sea fog veiled the woods, Ben was heard no more, and everyone knew he was dead.

What no one knew was how he'd died, *exactly*—and I was about to find out.

***

At my Boston apartment, my friends and I smashed into 2010 with a New Year's Eve session of *Cards Against Humanity*. On my turn, I called for a response to *Great in theory, messy in practice.*

My friend Suzanne had thrown down what I'd choose as the winner: *Dead parents.* We laugh-cried until mascara inched down our cheeks.

The others watched in the stone silence I'd expect at a funeral in which someone had just knocked over the casket. Only Suzanne knew that, even though I was in my thirties, all I'd wanted was to be plucked from the tar pit that was my childhood, and the last stuck limb was my mother's death.

It turned out I wouldn't have long to wait, but when that day came exactly ten months later, it was nothing like I'd imagined.

"Want me to go with?" My boyfriend Tom was propped against the damask headboard, naked, smoking a cigarette. He looked amazingly fresh considering we'd spent Halloween night at an open-bar costume ball and wildly unmasking each other between my sheets. "Looks like you could use company."

Yes! I wanted to cry, but we were still in that fabled Honeymoon period, when each was worthy of worship, when being together was magic, when every love song made sense and it was impossible not to obsess all day. It'd been going for almost a year, but he didn't know about my mother's Halloween histrionics, my weirdly overprotective Aunt Pia, the habits locals whispered about in the bars, the stares I got in the market.

I wasn't ready for *that* cranberry harvest just yet.

I opened the closet and dragged my soft traveler out from under a mountain of spike heels and boots. "No." I wrestled open the twisted, crushed bag. It smelled like old shoes. "I appreciate the offer, though."

"You're sure you're gonna be okay."

No. I hurried into the bathroom, arm-swept make-up from the vanity into the bag. "I'll be fine. I'll call you when I get settled there."

"Meena." He was the only one who called me that. Everyone else called me Jess; my full name was Jessamyn. He crushed his cigarette out in the ashtray. "You change your mind, call me. I'll get the next ferry."

"Okay." I set the bag on the bed. "I love you."

"I love you too."

We held each other's gazes for a moment, and the room was thick with his comforting smell, a little like bourbon and smoked applewood. It was the first time we'd said the L-word, but I couldn't do a happy dance about it. He looked hurt that I didn't, but there was just too much ahead of me.

Too much of what, exactly, I wasn't sure.

***

My mother's house was adjacent to the protected land where Booming Ben and the last of his kind used to live, its border a field of low-lying reddish scrub and grasses stretching to the coastline woods. There was a monument there instead—a hulking, six-foot high replica of Ben, his head cocked back, beak open in a silent cry—fashioned in black metal. It gleamed in the sun, but on foggy days, all anyone could see was a dark shape, looming in the mist.

No one had ever found Ben's body. It was almost as though he'd always been a ghost; that he and his species had never existed at all.

I navigated down lanes I'd rather not've, past houses still decorated for Halloween, the damp ocean air filling my car with the smell of salty dead leaves and mud.

There was a police car in the driveway, but I was more concerned with the condition of the Queen Anne I'd grown up in. It looked weary in its effort to cling to its majesty; the sea green exterior was chipped, the scalloped moldings were broken or missing, and the roof of its sagging porch bowed beneath a carpet of moss and weeds. Its once bright windows had been rendered blind due to sheets of moldering plywood; those were new since the last time I'd been there, four Thanksgivings ago. *So,* I thought, *Mom's insanity finally got to that point. I'm sure it gave the folks at Melchor's Hardware plenty of fresh gossip!*

Oddly, when I was a kid, I wasn't picked on too much. I think people felt pity for me, and girls with dysfunctional mothers always seem to get looked after by other women. I was invited to my fair share of birthday sleepovers, the school's Cupid Dance, afternoons at the beach, and the annual Lobster Bake. I also always had a ride to and from the church's Halloween Apple Bob—but that was the event I was never allowed to attend.

My mother was a skittish person who drifted through life wearing a haunted look. But she and my aunt were, for some reason, *terrified* to let me out of their sight on that night. Every Halloween, Mom locked herself in her bedroom and screamed into the wee hours, while Aunt Pia drank cup after cup of her homemade pumpkin sassafras tea at the kitchen table, did her crossword, and pretended she was deaf. Trick-or-treaters weren't welcome—there wasn't even a bowl of Smarties set out in a basket, and our porch light was always off.

I ascended the front steps. The screen door was warped and hit the frame with a *smack-shimmy,* and inside, the house reeked of mildew and rotten fruit. Dust floated in the only natural light that came from still-uncovered windows in the kitchen, and a single Tiffany lamp dimly revealed the living room's tattered drapes.

"Jess!" Mom's fraternal twin, Aunt Pia—a scrappy size one with a Brillo of dyed red hair—startled me from the shadows, her gaunt face wearing its usual pinched expression. She was the opposite of my tall, solid, round-faced mother, who'd worn her black hair in loose curls before it'd turned all white. It was sometimes hard to believe they were sisters.

She took off her reading glasses. "I doubted you'd come."

"Nice to see you, too." I set my handbag near the hall table, grateful it was too dark for me to gauge the dirty floors.

"It's been far too long." Pia turned and went into the kitchen.

I followed, noting the kitchen table, her crossword book next to a line of sharpened pencils, and a dirty dish crumbed with what'd probably been toast.

Pia seized the tea pot, filled it from the sink spigot. "It would've been nice for Helen to see you before she passed."

"I'm sorry. I just couldn't get here."

"I'm sure Boston's busy." She slammed the kettle on the stove and lit the burner. "I'm also sure that's not really the reason. But have some tea, because—" it came out *becaws*, something she'd picked up from years of housekeeping at a New Yorker's summer home "—Rusty's here and he's got questions for you."

I recalled the car in the driveway; she meant Officer Michael Skiff, but everyone'd called him Rusty. Even in this speck of a place, they didn't send a cop to every death, but I was glad it was him. He was the quiet, gentle guy the other girls never dated because he wasn't bad boy enough. But I'd liked that he'd always been good to me, so I'd said yes when he'd asked.

There were heavy footfalls on the stairs, which crackled in protest. I wondered if they were finally going to splinter in the middle.

"Hey, Jess." Rusty ducked through the kitchen arch so he didn't bump his head. "I'm real sorry."

I was tempted to fire, I'm *not,* but then it hit me that, former sweetheart or not, he *was* a cop, and that might be taken the wrong way.

"She's all yours," Pia said.

He reached into his pocket and extracted a sleek silver cell phone with a shiny olive back and a camera viewfinder. It was obviously newer than mine; I'd gotten my hot pink Motorola flip before the Thanksgiving trip home four years ago.

He looked at me. "I don't—I don't want to have to show you this, but this is just—we've never seen anything like it."

I could see pain and regret in his eyes. Had I been okay with living here the rest of my life, we probably would've gotten married; I think he knew that as well as I did. He pressed his lips together. "Just give me a minute."

I set my hand on his arm. His official issue jacket was cool under my fingers. "It's okay, Rust. I can handle it."

His big shoulders heaved as he took a deep breath and exhaled. He frowned, pushed small buttons on the phone, and passed it to me.

The photo was small and grainy, but it was my mother, in her bed, her fingers clutched around her stained comforter. Her face was swollen and blotched purple. Her lower jaw was unhinged. Her eyes were missing, just gaping black holes. Blood streaked her cheeks, rivered into her caverned mouth, unnaturally wide in a terrible, silent scream.

I wanted to burst into tears, but my knees buckled instead. Rusty caught my arm, settled me into one of the rickety kitchen chairs. It shifted under my weight.

He was quiet for a moment, his voice tentative and soft when he finally asked, "Do you know anything that might've caused that?"

I shook my head. "No."

"She didn't have any enemies, any—"

"I told you, I was home all night with her," Pia snapped.

"Aunt Pia. Please." I looked at Rusty. "No, she didn't."

"Could she have done this to herself?"

I couldn't imagine my mother stabbing out her eyes with—a knife? A fork? *God. Had it gotten* that *bad?* "Maybe? I don't know."

He responded with a serious, slow nod, presented his meaty palm for the phone. His hand was big enough to make it disappear. "Sorry I had to do that to you, but we had to ask."

"I get it. I'm okay." I'm not.

I want to throw up.

"I'll be in touch." He turned to leave.

Aunt Pia wasn't done.

"We need to make arrangements to bury her, now, you understand, don't you?" she said. "When are we going to be allowed to get that done?"

Rusty's eyes were full of apology. "A couple of days. The coron—I mean, *we*—just want to check some things out."

"I know my sister and I weren't the most popular people, but she still deserves a send-off like everyone else."

"We're just—we need to run some tests."

"I've already called Monk & Harris and we're trying to get something on the books."

"I'm going to get them to finish as quickly as they possibly can. I'm sure you won't have to wait a day or two more than's normal."

Pia folded her arms in front of her chest. "Look. She died in the middle of one of her screaming fits that was worse than usual. No one hurt her, no one poisoned her, nothing's going on here, and I don't understand why you think your—*tests*—are necessary—"

My patience was gone. "Aunt Pia, *please!*"

The tea kettle's shrill pierced the air. Pia rushed to stop it.

"She seemed perfectly healthy." Rusty looked beaten. "We just ... want a look-see."

"You do what you need to do," I said.

He nodded, and in a friendly gesture, patted my arm. "You need anything, Jess." He slid a sideways glance toward Pia. "You know where to find me."

"Thanks."

He showed himself out, closed the inner door behind him. The warped outer screen shimmied against the frame.

I let out an exasperated breath. "Did you really have to do that? He's only doing his job."

"She deserves a fair funeral. And the very suggestion that they think there was foul play here's hideously offensive."

"Seventy's still young. They just want to—determine— the cause of death. That's all." The image from the phone, tiny and grainy as it had been, scored my brain. "I've never seen anything like that, so *I'd* certainly like to know what caused it, and for once, can we make this about someone other than *you*?"

"All right." She slammed two saucers on the counter. "You want to know what caused it? I can *tell* you what caused it. Your mother was *riddled* with guilt. *That's* what." She yanked a pair of familiar china cups from the cupboard. "She did herself in, letting it eat away at her soul like that."

"Quit being cryptic and just tell me."

Aunt Pia was quiet as she filled our teacups. She brought them to the table and sat down across from me.

"We were sixteen. Momma had just died and Daddy'd bought a new Fairlane. Your mother was dying to take it for spin—she had a boyfriend, was teaching her how to drive. One of the Tilton boys, I think." She steeped a teabag. "Halloween night, your grandfather came home from the Apple Bob, drunk as hell. Passed out in this very living room, and Helen took his keys. I warned her not to, but she wouldn't listen, of course, and I couldn't let her go alone."

"She barely knew what she was doing. In all my life I was never so scared. It was foggy, but she managed to miss the hordes of trick-or-treating Davy Crocketts and Cinderellas." She dropped three sugar cubes in her cup, stirred with a spoon. "But then, something small and brown and quick darted out of that mist. We didn't feel much more than a bump."

Oh my God.

"It could've been grouse or pheasant. It wasn't. We knew it was Booming Ben." She took a sip of her tea.

My legs went leaden.

"Helen just stood there in the headlights, staring. She wanted the police. But I knew what bad thing we'd done. I grabbed Ben by his feet, hurled him into the woods. Made her vow we'd never tell a soul. We never did."

Pia looked drained. Tired.

Old.

She set her cup on its saucer. "The next year, that's when Helen started screaming. Every Halloween. For decades. Believed the angry spirits of those poor, extinct hens were coming after her. That's why your father left, and then she was convinced they were coming to get you, too, and that's why we couldn't let you out on that night."

My chest felt heavy.

"She never got over it."

I wasn't so sure I was going to get over it, either—the photo, the confession, the *answers*. My mother had been in a living hell. Right across the hall.

But all I had to do was bury her and go home, and then I would be unstuck.

Right?

"Truth be told, I was glad you went to Boston." There was a glimmer of regret in her eyes, which also seemed, for the first time ever, damp. "I wasn't expected to keep you from your fun anymore."

She sniffed, got up and padded into the tiny bathroom under the stairs.

I swore I heard her crying.

They didn't find anything suspicious, but I knew they wouldn't. The funeral was a few days later, and I was surprised at how many people *were* there—Pastor Luce and a couple of parishioners, Aunt Pia's Friday night pinochle circle, John Pease the postman, Mrs. Ripley the librarian, and Rusty.

When I got back to Boston, my first stop was at Tom's apartment. I dropped my bag in his entranceway and burst into tears.

He immediately took me in his arms. "It's okay, you

know," he said. "You wanna cry it all out, you go ahead."

But I knew no amount of crying in the world was going to get it out of me.

***

The next September, Tom and I bought a condo together in the Back Bay. It was a baby-shake of a place that needed work—replacing the old carpets with hardwoods for starters. But we wanted to be in a trendy area, and that was what we could do on our salaries. Beyond the logistics of painting and updating, of shedding *mine* and buying *ours*, our other priority was preparing for the Halloween ball—something that'd taken a back seat since we'd been house hunting. We settled on Henry Miller and Anaïs Nin—I even dusted my hair gold and wore a bird cage on my head.

We won the costume contest, and had planned to spend the entirety of All Saints' Day in bed, ordering in, and sipping hair-of-the-dog champagne while maxxing ourselves out on horror movies.

It didn't go as planned. At six o'clock in the morning, Pastor Luce called from Martha's Vineyard to tell me Aunt Pia was dead.

***

Despite my protests, Tom went with me. Packed our bags, made the ferry reservation, drove us to Wood's Hole.

The elderly Queen Anne had decayed even further. One of the porch awning supports had actually broken, so the roof not only bowed, it pitched. Pieces of molding littered the leaf-blanketed lawn. The stoop stairs were splintered, and not one window wasn't plastered over with plywood.

Fear shot through me when I saw Rusty's police car in the driveway.

Tom kissed the back of my hand. "It'll be fine."

No. No it would not.

I knew what was waiting.

Outside was a warmish November afternoon, but inside was a damp, chilly evening. Slivers of the gray day forced themselves around the edges of the plywood, the only other illumination from the Tiffany lamps in the living room, where Rusty and Pastor Luce were seated. When I came in, they rose to their feet and offered their condolences; I introduced Tom.

It clearly set Rusty on edge. "Look, I hate to do this to you again, but—" Unlike a year ago, he held out the phone with no fanfare, no pain, no regret.

I couldn't bear it. I looked away.

Tom didn't, and was instantly sickened. "Jesus *Christ*."

"Just seems a little odd, is all, and one year to the day."

Tom got in his face. "What are you implying? Meena had something to do with that?" Rusty looked confused. "Meena."

"Jess," I said. "They only know me as Jess, here, Tom."

Tom turned and stared at me, looking betrayed.

I shrugged. "I was a different person then." I wasn't. When I'd moved to Boston, *that's* when I started pretending I was a different person.

"Not at all, sir." Rusty slipped the phone back in his pocket. His official issue jacket looked a little worn. "We're just thinking she can help us."

It was burn or be burnt. I approached Rusty, set my hands on his. "Listen, can I please have a couple of minutes with Pastor Luce? I just—I just need a few."

I see an uncharacteristic flash of anger. "You *do* know something."

"I didn't last year. But I might now. I—I need a little time, okay? Can you step out?"

Rusty looked frustrated. "You really have to talk to me, Jess."

"I will. I promise. Just ... *please*."

He took a deep breath, eyed Tom with a grimace, and made his exit.

"What was that all about?"

"Tom, just sit."

"But—"

"Sit *down*." I reminded myself of Aunt Pia.

Tom sat on the couch.

I suddenly realized that the dump we were sitting in belonged to me. It'd been in our family for generations, but my only plan for it was a bulldozer.

Or a match.

Pastor Luce settled on a threadbare wing-backed chair. A welter of dust puffed into the air and drifted into the light of the side table's Tiffany. "Your Aunt Pia ... she called me last night. Begged me to come, but I was with— old Mr. Tilton's family. He was dying. I couldn't leave. So I sent Rusty. When he got here, he found ... well ... you know. But Jess, Pia told me ... everything."

I sank to the couch.

"Meena, what is it?" Tom's voice was tinged with annoyance. "Would somebody please tell me what the *hell* is going on here?"

"My mother died the same way." I lowered my voice, then, and quietly shared details of Booming Ben's demise and my mother's belief that she was haunted. Only enough to satisfy him, though—he didn't need to know the embarrassing parts, about the screaming, about how terrible my childhood had been because of it.

When it was over, Tom reached over and squeezed my hand.

"There's something your aunt wanted me to share with you." Pastor Luce leaned forward. "She kept saying that it was real. That they were coming for her. And that once she was gone, they were going to come for you."

I felt punched in the gut. "Oh, no. Absolutely not. That was all in their heads. Delusions. Both of them."

"She said that's what she'd thought about your mother. She understood that she was wrong. It's why she begged me to come. She wanted absolution."

"This is ridiculous." I sprung from the couch. "They don't exist, and even if they *did*, no dead bird spirits are going to *stalk* me for something that happened years before I was born!" I needed air. I stormed outside.

"She wanted me to warn you." The pastor called. "It's real and it's not going to stop."

I burst onto the porch, nearly crashing into Rusty, who'd clearly been listening by the door. The temperature had dropped by at least twenty degrees, and a moist, frigid wind stung my cheek.

"You okay?" Rusty asked.

Tom emerged. "She's fine."

It was clear Rusty'd had enough. "Far be it from me, sir." He gave me a wounded look, got into his car, and drove away.

After the sound of Rusty's engine had faded, there was an eerie silence, a gloom. I looked down the driveway, out at the lane, the road I'd stared at every day of my childhood, wondering when the last time would be I'd see it from that perspective. That moment was it. But something, for certain, was very *present*. "Give me a butt."

Surprised, he hesitated—he knew I'd quit smoking years ago. But he reached into his pocket, lit a cigarette, and passed it to me. "Listen, sweetie. I'm sure it's—I'm sure it's all just bullshit. Creepy stories. He's wrong."

I took a long, soothing drag, then flicked the ash into the dead beach rose bush. "What if he's not?"

***

We buried Aunt Pia in our family plot at Old Westside Cemetery. My grandparents were on one side, Mom and my own, unoccupied grave on the other; I suppressed an ominous shudder every time my eyes drifted toward its undisturbed grass.

I forced myself not to think about it.

Great in theory, messy in practice.

Like my mother and Pia had their plywood on the Queen Anne, I had a bolted door in my mind. Behind it, I put my past. Sometimes, though, in bed at night, lying in Tom's arms while he slept after making love, the bolt unlatched and memories slithered out.

The sound of my mother's screams. The smell of mildew and rotten fruit. The taste of Aunt Pia's pumpkin sassafras tea. The view of the lane from the porch. The feel of Rusty's official issue jacket; the dank sea air on my cheek. *And once she was gone, they were going to come for you.*

I doubled my efforts. I made plans to raze the house, sell the land.

"If you wanna go back there and get some things, we can." Tom used chopsticks to manipulate lo mein as we sat at our new tiled dinette.

"I have everything I want." Which was nothing.

"No photos, even?"

"I don't even think there were any." It was true. I didn't recall ever having seen any, not even of my grandparents, who were both dead before I was born.

He eyed me strangely.

"You saw the condition that stuff was in."

"True."

I reached across the table and set my hand on his. "My life is *here*," I said. "*Completely*, and with *you*."

Just like every night, he took me to bed and we made love. Just like every night, I lie in his arms afterward, and just like every night, out they slithered, my mother's screams ... *once she was gone, they were going to come for you*, cycling until dawn.

It will stop when the house is gone.

It didn't.

It will stop when the land is sold.

It didn't.

I wasn't feeling well for a couple of weeks.

On Mother's Day, we found out I was pregnant.

We hung an Audubon calendar on the freshly-painted kitchen wall. We put my appointments on it, numbering the Sundays—*Wk 4, Wk 16, Wk 28*—and marking my due date with a star.

Tom was thrilled at the prospect of being a father.

I wasn't so sure I wanted to be a mother, especially when each week guaranteed a fresh hell: The morning queasiness that eventually gave way to nausea and throwing up at any hour. Overwhelming odors, like the stink of rotten mangoes. A taste in my mouth like pennies. Constantly, desperately needing to pee. Sore, heavy, enlarging breasts. Exhaustion. Nasal congestion. Headaches. Nosebleeds. Excruciating leg cramps. Shortness of breath. A swelling abdomen.

With each new horror came the question, *Is this what my mother felt when she was pregnant with me?* The worse everything got, the more guilt that I'd failed to understand her, grown to hate her, then abandoned her.

During *Wk 20*, we learned we were having a girl. Inside

me, she already had vocal chords, teeth, and fingerprints, could recognize my voice, and was the size of a banana. We called her Aura.

Six weeks later, she was the size of a cauliflower, could hear the outside world, and kicked. My back ached relentlessly and I had to jam cloths into my new, enormous bras to catch leakage. My feet and hands were swollen, I was constipated—but having trouble controlling my frequent, urgent peeing—and my belly made every movement a chore.

Our building's rooftop garden had an awning area with cushioned rocking chairs that were easy to get in and out of. Feeling ill and needing air, I discovered that sitting in one relieved the pressure on my pelvis and eased my back.

It was the first time I noticed the doves.

Not like I hadn't seen them—we lived in a city; pigeons and mourning doves were as ubiquitous as the Swan Boats in the Public Garden during the summer.

On the street, they were skittish—get near them, and they took off with a *whinny-doo* and hard-beating wings. But the teeming, bobbing mass approached, got close enough that I heard their feet make tap-scratches on the concrete, got a deep look in their eyes—dull, black pearls ringed in white.

It was like a thousand small eclipses, watching me.

They *whoove-whooved* a call that people who didn't know better mistook for owls. It reminded me of something, but my pregnancy brain couldn't figure out what.

"Shoo!" I kicked a swollen leg.

They advanced.

"Get out of here!"

They kept coming.

They spooked me.

I hauled myself up and moved as fast as I could to the rooftop door, wrestled it open.

The doves pursued.

I slipped inside, pulled the door closed behind me with a *bang-click*. The automatic halogens come on, flooded the stairwell in a harsh, buzzing white light.

I heard the doves cry. I figured out what their *whoove-whoove* reminded me of.

Someone blowing over the mouth of a beer bottle.

Booming Ben burst into my mind.

I'm sure it's all just bullshit. Creepy stories. He's wrong, Tom had said that last day at the house.

Of *course* Pastor Luce was wrong.

But what if he wasn't?

I stroked my burgeoning bump. If he *wasn't* wrong, was I going to do to Aura what my mother had done to me?

Would she grow to hate me?

Was Tom going to leave me, like my dad?

Something wet and warm ran down my legs, into my sneakers, welled up, puddled on the stair.

I'd peed.

Back in the condo, after I'd cleaned myself up, all I could see was the calendar and its countdown numbers in red hearts. My pregnancy was more than halfway done, thank God. But something loomed in between my current misery and the blissful relief of Aura's arrival.

Halloween.

***

"We should go to the ball this year if you're up to it," Tom said one morning when Aura was the size of an eggplant, my belly felt especially tight, and I hadn't gotten much sleep.

I'd forgotten about the ball, and no, I probably wasn't going to be physically up to it, but a taste of my old life, even for a couple of hours, sounded refreshing.

"Got a great idea for a costume. You can be the sun. Put you in a gold robe, paint a stylized face and rays on your belly." He poured coffee into his silver travel mug. "I'll be Icarus. Use the old sheers we ripped off the bedroom windows and wire for wings."

Wings.

I remembered what Aunt Pia had said: *That's why we couldn't let you out on that night ...*

What if we were at the party and I heard them coming? The *whooving* of hundreds of breaths over empty bottles, the scratching of thousands of scurrying hen's feet, the beating of millions of ruffling feathers?

I'd be as vulnerable as a chick in a fox's hen house.

I looked at the calendar.

Seven days until October 31.

Seven.

On Halloween morning, our costumes were hangered on the shower rod. They were exquisite, artful—the shiny gold robe, painted with a sun where my belly would be, with its frown and rouged cheeks; the sheers of Tom's wings, spray-painted to intimate ghostly, burnt feathers.

We'd have won that year.

But we weren't going.

I needed to protect Aura. I was going to end it. So she'd never hear me scream. She'd never miss trick-or-treating. She'd never wonder if Booming Ben and his spectral brood were going to come for her.

How I was going to do this was another issue.

We had boards. Stacks of gorgeous, three-inch-wide maple we'd chosen for the dining room floor.

I lifted them—a challenge given my physical tortures—and dragged them to our bedroom. I got Tom's hammer, but had trouble choosing the most appropriate nails from the tool chest. Finally, I just grabbed the longest ones.

I went to the hutch and pulled out the mahogany box that held our silver carving set, the one we'd purchased in anticipation of our first Thanksgiving in the condo. My suffering had thwarted our plans to have the dining room in order for that day, but the large knife and serving fork were sharp and at the ready.

Just in case.

I locked myself in our bedroom. It was slow, painful, and I had to take frequent breaks, but I hammered boards across the door. I hammered boards over the windows. I even hammered boards over the closets.

Then, I waited. I sat in the corner, leaned against the wall, set my hand protectively over Aura. She kicked. I recalled a song my mother had sung to me: "Feed the Birds."

I sang it to her.

I listened. I sang. I used our master bathroom every thirty minutes.

The hours passed.

I'd forgotten about Tom until I heard him come home. "Meena?"

I went quiet. I heard him rummage in the kitchen; heard the refrigerator open, then close.

"Meena, where are you?"

The bedroom door handle shimmied. "Meena?" He cursed. Knocked. "Are you okay? What's going on? Are you in there?"

I shifted. I needed to pee again, but I could feel them, coming.

I wet myself.

"Open this door!"

I didn't respond.

"Meena!" He banged with his fists. "Sweetie, let me *in!*"

I couldn't. I was *bound* to hear them any minute, the *whooving* of hundreds of breaths over empty bottles, the scratching of thousands of scurrying hen's feet, the beating of millions of ruffling feathers.

My blood curdled, and I started to scream. Because Tom knew the story of Booming Ben—the last living heath hen on the planet. He even knew how he'd died, *exactly*.

But there was a lot he didn't know. He didn't know about the screaming, every Halloween night, for decades. He didn't know who I was to become—a skittish, haunted wisp, drifting through life.

He didn't know about what this would make me do to Aura.

I wrapped my hands around the knife and fork, because I wasn't going to let him find out.

The Boy Who Drowned On Dry Land
Marlin Bressi

There are many deep dives along the waterfront that are suitable for a good sloshing, but if you really want to be entertained, come down to McGinty's Pub on any given Thursday night and listen to the motley assemblage of old rivermen and retired ironworkers who sit like gargoyles in the back booth where the warm glow of the neon sign never reaches.

We call ourselves the Wharf Rats, and since we spend every night of the week here at Walter McGinty's humble establishment reminiscing about life and heartbreak to the lonesome toots of the barges chugging along the Ohio, we decided not too long ago that one night a week ought to be dedicated to something else entirely-- and that is how the Thursday Night Whopper Topper Club came into being.

For the uninitiated-- which I suppose includes everybody on God's green earth except for yours truly and my six fellow Wharf Rats-- the club was founded out of a fellow's natural inclination to boast and brag, to tell a whopper of a tale taller than the one he had just heard. The fellow who spins the best yarn is rewarded with a pitcher of Iron City's finest pilsner, which may not be as good as Milwaukee's finest, but it gets the job done.

One Thursday evening, about a month ago, Big Lou suggested that our weekly topic ought to be the otherworldly and macabre. I suppose we had all grown a little tired of comparing medical maladies and bragging-- or lying outright-- about the size of fish we had caught and so, by unanimous decision, we agreed to venture into darker waters. Besides, Lou had brought a glass vial into McGinty's the week before containing a kidney stone so big that it made you hurt just looking at it. He showed off his mineral concretion to anyone who wanted to have a look, with the pride of a Yukon prospector showing off a gold nugget.

There was plenty of talk about haunted iron furnaces that evening, of headless apparitions wandering the Pennsy Railroad tracks beneath the silvery light of the full moon, and tales of Ouija boards and demented hermits and sad-sack holiday suicides who leaped from the Hot Metal Bridge into the icy Monongahela, but all of these stories were old hat to us; we had been spooking each other since childhood with these familiar yarns and it appeared there wasn't a Wharf Rat among us who had anything particularly unusual to offer in the way of mysterious fare. Frankly, it seemed that nobody was likely to quench his thirst with a pitcher of Iron City's finest on this particular evening.

That is, until Harry Esterhazy spoke up.

Thing about Harry is that he's a swell chap. Got all the respectability that a son of a Hungarian immigrant could hope for, and more friends than he can shake a stick at. Plus, he was a damn fine construction foreman to boot. A real swell guy, just like I said. But ever since that night down at McGinty's, none of us Wharf Rats have been able to look at him the same way. Matter of fact, he kind of makes the temperature of our blood drop a few degrees whenever he walks through the door.

Poor sap never should've opened his mouth. But he did, and it all began like this:

"My little brother Nicholas was quite young when he died in 1925. Although we were born and raised in the city, Papa would drive us over to Johnstown each summer and drop us off at Aunt Vanda's place, where we would spend a few weeks while Papa and his buddies went up to Lake Ontario, where one of the fellows had a cabin. Aunt Vanda's house was up on Prospect Hill, which is about a quarter mile north of downtown. It was a big, sprawling house with a wonderful view of the city below, but the house was always in a state of disrepair. Are you sure I haven't told you fellows about how my brother Nicky died?"

As he stopped to pour himself a splash of whiskey we all shook our heads and eagerly implored him to continue.

"Very well," he said, taking a swig of the amber liquid before wiping his moistened lips with a flannel sleeve. "Nicholas was obsessed with all thing aeronautical," explained Harry, running a thick, stubby finger along the rim of his glass, as if trying to produce a musical note. "He loved blimps, zeppelins and airplanes equally. He was spellbound by rockets and missiles. If it sailed, whizzed or floated through the air, my little brother was fascinated by it. He especially loved to fly kites, and Nicky had amassed quite an impressive collection before he died at the tender age of twelve.

"It was a breezy day in the middle of June and we had been at Aunt Vanda's place for nearly a week when Nicky decided to take Aunt Vanda's dog-- a wiry little terrier with a black and tan coat-- and leave the house on Prospect Hill to fly his newest kite in a clearing on the hilltop above Johnstown, not far from where William Penn Avenue runs. Back in those days I believe it was known as the Old Ebensburg Road. I accompanied Nicholas to the clearing, but, as I wasn't much for kite flying, I soon lost interest and returned to Aunt Vanda's house. That was the last time I saw my brother alive."

At this point in the story Harry looked up from his empty glass and called out to Walter McGinty, the ancient proprietor, to bring him something stronger. McGinty hobbled over with a bottle of gin bearing a shabby label that give the impression that its contents may or may not have been manufactured in somebody's bathtub.

Harry poured from the bottle and mumbled a few sentences about his aunt; I believe her last name might have been Namath, or possibly Nemeth. She had come over from Hungary around the turn of the century with her husband, who died in a coal mine less than a year later, which explained why the house was in a constant state of disrepair. His aunt and uncle did not speak fluent English, Harry explained; as a result, their last name was spelled a variety of different ways in family records. It was the typical immigrant's tale.

"When night came and neither Nicky nor the dog had returned to the house, Aunt Vanda grew worried and implored me to go out and look for them," continued Harry. "I grabbed my uncle's lantern and set off for the clearing, and I returned to the house less than twenty minutes later, white as a sheet and crying uncontrollably, accompanied by an old man. The old man, you see, was the night caretaker at the St. Petka Serbian cemetery, which was located just down the street from the house, and Aunt Vanda assumed that I was crying because I had gotten yelled at by the caretaker for trespassing. But this was not the case."

The old caretaker, whose name escaped Harry, explained to the bewildered aunt that he had seen a teenage boy carrying a lantern through the woods above the cemetery and, concerned for his safety, abandoned his post to investigate. The woods around Johnstown were no place for a child to ramble about, not with the abundance of forgotten mineshafts and ore pits. When the caretaker finally caught up with the youth he encountered a ghastly sight: Lying in a clearing in the woods, illuminated by the warm yellow glow of the kerosene lamp, was the limp body of a small boy with a tiny dog sprawled beside him. The boy's brand new kite dangled from the brack of a nearby tree, twisting in the breeze. "They both appeared to be dead," said Harry. "I had never seen a dead body, of course, but the moment I lifted my lantern to Nicky's face I knew that he had been snatched away from the realm of the living. There wasnt a scratch on him, and it may have appeared to others that he was sleeping, but a boy knows the face of his own brother better than anyone else-- knows it better than even the mother and father. And I knew just by looking at him that something had gone terribly wrong."

Harry developed a misty, faraway look in his eye and turned toward the window. He suspended his story just long enough to watch the lights of a coal barge drift by. It sounded its horn in the darkness, gently rattling the windowpane with its cry.

"I was hysterical when I came across the bodies, as you could imagine," he finally continued, "and so the caretaker carried me in his arms back to Aunt Vanda's house and then hurried down the hill to notify the police. An officer arrived about an hour later, accompanied by the coroner. They retrieved the bodies from the clearing and took them downtown to the morgue.

"An autopsy was performed on little Nicky, and it revealed that my little brother had drowned-- on dry land! Surely this must be some kind of mistake, or so my family thought-- for the weather had been absolutely gorgeous and it had not rained in days-- and so the chief of police, at my mother's insistence, ordered the coroner to perform an autopsy on the dog as well. The coroner must have thought the police of chief had gone mad, but he shrugged and did as he was told. Once again, the cause of death was determined to be drowning.

"It was certainly strange, the coroner said, but not impossible. He told my mother about a rare phenomenon called dry drowning, which can occur days after a victim has gone swimming and has gotten water in the lungs. After a few days the fluid buildup causes uncontrollable spasms and the airway constricts." Harry admitted that he had indeed gone swimming with Nicholas the previous afternoon in the shallow creek behind Prospect Hill, but insisted that the dog had not accompanied them. Of this detail he was quite certain.

"Even though the coroner's theory did not explain how the terrier had died, my family accepted the explanation. As for myself, however, I was not convinced." Harry once again paused to look out the window. I looked at Big Lou, whose mouth was open as if he were about to speak, but he thought better of it and waited, like the rest of us, for Harry to continue his tale. "At any rate, my brother's body was prepared for burial by a Johnstown undertaker, and the tiny coffin was put on a train and sent back to Pittsburgh and buried in a churchyard a few miles outside the city," he continued. "The following year Aunt Vanda passed away and the house on Prospect Hill was sold to another family. I haven't been back to Johnstown since."

I could tell that I wasn't the only Wharf Rat who felt slightly cheated by the story. True, it was sad-- perhaps even a little mysterious-- but I asked Harry how drowning on dry land could possibly be interpreted as otherworldly. He glanced up from his glass of gin and called out to the ancient barkeep. McGinty flung his rag over his shoulder and ambled over to the booth.

"Walter, you were born and raised in Johnstown, right?" asked Harry. "How much do you know about the flood?"

"Which one?" asked the bartender in a sarcastic tone. There were many to choose from: 1906, 1907, 1936, and the Big One. We all understood that Harry was talking about the 1899 flood, of course, which claimed so many lives that, even today, historians still can't agree on the exact number of dead. For years afterward bodies were found, some hundreds of miles away, carried downriver by the current.

"Which one? The one that killed over two thousand people!" I interrupted with an edge of impatience in my voice. It was getting late and I knew that my wife was already waiting for me at home with a prepared lecture. McGinty said that, yes, he knew all about the Great Flood of 1899. In fact, he had been one of the survivors.

"Do you know about Camp Hastings?" asked Harry. "And Grandview Cemetery?"

"What's to know?" replied the bartender dispassionately. "About eight hundred of the unidentified victims were buried in the Plot of the Unknowns at Grandview Cemetery. Everyone in western Pennsylvania knows that. They teach it in history class. Teachers take children there for field trips."

"But what about Camp Hastings?" prodded Harry. The bartender closed his eyes and wrinkled his forehead in thought, trying to recall a place that barely warrants a mention in history textbooks.

"Yeah, I know something about that place," answered McGinty. "The way I remember it, the army came and set up a camp on Prospect Hill after the flood. They buried hundreds of victims in shallow makeshift graves up on the hillside, near the Old Ebensburg Road, until a permanent burial ground could be established. No one had ever planned for a disaster of that magnitude, and there was no other place to put the bodies. Because of the heat and the fear of contagious disease, the victims had be covered up in a hurry. I remember climbing up the hill from the back with a couple of friends, trying to sneak a peek at the gravediggers at work, but the guards always caught us and shooed us away. But the stench-- why, that is something that will haunt me until my dying day."

"Rather a macabre way for a boy to spend an afternoon, eh, Wally?" asked Big Lou. The bartender threw his head back and laughed.

"This was long before that idiot contraption they call television came along," he replied. "Long before comic strips and radio programs. You had to get your kicks wherever you could find them."

"Surely you remember hearing about the dogs?" asked Harry.

"The dogs? What dogs?" asked McGinty, just before his face lit up with a sudden flicker of remembrance, as if the details of a forgotten dream had suddenly materialized inside his mind. "That's right, I had almost forgotten! You see, the guards at Camp Hastings had a devil of a time keeping the dogs away. The mutts were constantly disturbing the shallow graves-- digging them open and devouring the corpses."

The Wharf Rats grimaced and stuck out their tongues in a unified display of disgust. Pete, the most royally whiskered rat among us, upped the ante by producing a guttural, retching sound. The bartender rolled his eyes and shook his head.

"Well, who do you suppose was left after the flood to feed the dogs, Pete?" asked McGinty. This was something I had never thought about, and these are the minor details to which nobody gives any thought in the maddening, desperate hours and days following a terrible disaster. All creatures, great and small, will do whatever they have to in order to survive. McGinty recalled that the guards at Camp Hastings were forced to shoot over a hundred of the starving mongrels during the course of a single night.

"Nobody in town slept a wink that night," said the bartender. "Just as soon as you'd feel yourself drift off to sleep, a volley of rifle shots would scare the devil out of you. And that howling! It was enough to chill you to the core. It was a terrible, ghastly thing."

McGinty shook his head and hobbled back to the bar, and I stared at Harry Esterhazy with eyes that could finally see why he refused to believe the coroner's theory about dry drowning. I wouldn't have believed the coroner's explanation either. The black and tan terrier was the key to the tale.

"The restless spirits of Johnstown were still angry about having their corpses devoured by dogs," I announced for the benefit of any Wharf Rat who didn't understand, "and so, when a young boy and his terrier trod the sacred ground, the nameless dead reached out from beyond the grave and exacted their revenge!"

Harry nodded, and I felt a sudden shiver race up my spine. What would have happened to Harry if he had decided not to abandon his brother in the clearing on Prospect Hill? Would he have suffered the same strange and tragic fate? For that matter, what exactly *had* happened to Nicholas and Aunt Vanda's wire-haired terrier on that terrible evening? What had they seen? Was it a thousand vaporous, ethereal arms reaching up from the desecrated soil? A parade of bloated, restless phantoms with anger burning brightly in the blank spaces where their eyes had once been? Or was the act of otherworldly revenge invisible, as subtle as a gasp for air, as silent as a whisper, as sudden as a heart attack?

I concluded that nothing rising up from the forgotten burial ground on Prospect Hill could have been as terrible as the guilt that Harry had been forced to live with for all of these years for leaving little Nicky Esterhazy alone in that wretched clearing. A quick and painless death-- at least in my opinion-- would have been preferable to shouldering a psychological boulder the size of Everest.

I said as much to my stone-faced companions and they grumbled in agreement, except for Pete, whose twitchy moustache and loud belching suggested that he had his doubts about the veracity of Harry's story. Sensing this skepticism, Harry reached into the pocket of his trousers and produced his worn brown leather wallet. He withdrew a small, rectangular piece of thin, stamped metal which, like all us Wharf Rats, had seen better days. After he placed the rusted 1925 dog tag on the table we had no choice but to call McGinty over to the booth and ask him to bring our friend a pitcher of Iron City's finest pilsner, which may not be as good as the pilsner they have in Milwaukee, but it gets the job done.

Breathers
Guy Belleranti

the
hot
heavy
breathing on
the back of my neck
unnerves me and I run, fearing
it will soon be joined
by the ice
cold breath
of
death

Evidence of the Eternal
Jonah Mason

"When did you start hearing the voices?"

Gregory Exeter stared out the window that screened the psychiatrist's office from the building standing within twelve feet of where he sat. He could see himself in the pane's reflection, a silhouette in shadow and light superimposed on the outside world.

"Mr. Exeter?"

He snapped back into the office. "I'm sorry. What?"

"You came to me saying you were bothered by voices. When did you start hearing them?" Dr. Ellen Stuart repeated. She tapped her pen against her desktop idly, her green eyes watching him closely from below her graying hair bound in a tight bun. Exeter smiled apologetically. He had a nice smile, one that actually reached his eyes. She was so used to people who smiled insincerely that it often took her by surprise when she met someone who genuinely smiled. Exeter's folder might have said he was over sixty, but his whole being seemed younger. Her first impression had been he was just under forty. The clean-shaven face, the mane of jet-black hair untouched by gray, the grace of a man half his age, all combined to give him a much younger appearance.

"Bothered? I don't know if I'd call it being bothered. More like concerned. I guess I was about twelve when Andrew started talking to me," he told her. "Martha first spoke to me on my twenty-fifth birthday. As for the others, well," he shrugged, "I really can't say. Some I think I've heard since I was little, others I'm just now starting to hear."

She frowned at him and switched to tapping her front tooth with the pen. "So, you're hearing new voices now," she prompted.

He nodded. "Oh, yes. Almost daily. Yesterday, a voice introducing itself as Doug spoke to me," he went on. "He's different than any voice I've heard so far. I guess I've been expecting to hear from him, or someone like him, though."

"Really? How?"

Exeter was struggling for the right words. Dr. Stuart waited patiently as he stood and began to pace the length of her office, his long legs striding quickly back and forth.

"He's more knowledgeable than the others," he went on, as if not hearing her question. "He seems better informed."

"About what?"

Exeter waved his hands vaguely. "Everything. Especially about me."

Dr. Stuart nodded. "And that makes you uncomfortable," she suggested.

He stopped pacing and looked at her blankly. "No. Why should it?"

The psychiatrist shifted in her seat. "Well, some people feel it's an unacceptable invasion of privacy for someone to know so much."

Exeter resumed pacing. "Oh, no. It doesn't bother me. It's just, he seems to know so much, but he won't tell me the things I want to know."

"Things...?"

"Well, like, do I ever win the lottery? How successful will I become?" He seemed drawn again to the window. "When will I die?"

"Excuse me, but I have to ask," the doctor interrupted. "How is Doug supposed to know all this?"

Exeter smiled at her and walked to the window to look outside. For a long moment he stood quietly watching. "There's something I haven't told you, doc."

"Yes?"

"These voices I hear --- Andrew, John, Martha, Robert, Phillip, even Doug --- they're all me."

Dr. Stuart scratched a note. "Excellent. I think we're making definite progress, Greg. That you realize these voices are internal is a major step."

"It's not just that they're internal, doc," Exeter stopped her. He stepped away from the window and regarded her silently for a moment before walking to the desk and sitting on its edge.

"Do you believe in reincarnation?"

Exeter's question took Dr. Stuart by surprise, though she would never admit it. As a matter of fact, she was a recent Hindu convert, something she had not discussed with any of her patients. She was still concerned that such a revelation might lose her some of her more conventionally minded clients. Momentarily, she had an anxious moment wondering if Exeter was toying with her, seeing how she might react at his knowledge of her secret. But, then, Exeter was going on as if the question were already answered.

"I'm not sure I do, myself, but..." He stopped and picked up a ball point pen from her desk. "Let's say you have a man. His name is Joe." Exeter indicated the pen. "Is what makes up Joe on the outside or the inside, or is it a combination of both?"

She looked at the pen and back to him. "What do you think?"

Exeter smiled at her question. "Don't want to commit, eh? Can't say I blame you." He gazed at the pen for a moment, as if considering its existence. "When Joe dies," and here he unscrewed the barrel of the pen, parting it into its components and removing the ink cartridge, "is that the end of Joe? When the outside expires, does the inside go with it?" He looked at the ink cartridge closely. "If the inside doesn't go with it, if it really existed, where did it go?"

She watched him as he pondered his own question. It was obvious he was performing something he had done several times before. For himself? For someone else?

He finally seemed to come to a conclusion. "It goes back into itself, doc. It returns to itself and then finds a new --- outlet, if you will."

"You're talking about transmigration of souls, the movement of a soul from body to body through multiple lifetimes," she said. "Reincarnation, transmigration, they're pretty much the same essentially."

He raised at eyebrow at her cynically. "Do you have another pen?"

It took her a second to grasp the question, then she opened the center drawer and pulled out another ball point to hand to him. He quickly broke it open and slipped the first pen's ink cartridge inside the barrel, then regarded the two brass tubes sticking out of the barrel.

"Don't all pens come with an ink cartridge already installed?" he asked her.

She caught the inference. "You think that these voices you're hearing are the dead trying to inhabit your body?" she asked quietly. It was possible Exeter was more ill than she had realized.

Exeter frowned at her, then his eyes wandered away to the window again. "Well, yes and no."

"Yes and no?"

He hefted his weight off the desk and walked to the window. She couldn't help noticing that he seemed drawn to the window the way a moth is drawn to a flame, seemingly without the will to stop. She was suddenly aware of the six-floor drop to the alleyway outside. With an effort, she kept to her own seat. It wouldn't be wise to precipitate something he might not actually be considering.

"They are all me, past and present, and now, in Doug, future. Doug is me, or that part of me that is not physical, but in the future."

Dr. Stuart thought about that for a second, then made a note of it. It could be an indication of a coming crisis. When she looked back at Exeter, he was gazing out the window again. She knew she should wait until pressure of speech prompted him to resume the conversation, but then she knew that wouldn't work. He seemed to carry on a continual internal dialog with his voices.

"Mr. Exeter?"

He seemed to come back from far away and politely turned to her.

"How do you think it's possible that Doug should be in the future and here as well?" she asked.

Exeter's forehead creased, and he seemed to listen for a moment. "Bilocation," he said at last. "There have been many reports of people seeing loved ones at the moment of their death hundreds of miles away. Bilocation negates time as well as space." Again, he was drawn to the window. "The evidence of the eternal," he murmured. Standing, he approached the glass.

Unreasoning anxiety brought Dr. Stuart out from behind her desk to place herself between him and the window.

"Greg, I'm having a little trouble sorting this out," she said, putting a bit of pressure on his forearm to move him away from the window. "What do you mean by 'evidence of the eternal'?"

He didn't resist her guiding him across the room to sit by her desk. He seemed not to notice either her nervousness or his own actions, staring vacantly ahead.

"What does it mean, 'eternal'?" he asked the air before him. "How do we conceive time? We see a linear set of cause and effect events and call their order 'time'. We mark the relative motions of planetary bodies to calibrate that order. We use 'time' to calibrate, measure, and define 'time' without realizing how insubstantial it really is. It remains merely a description of a perception, not a reality."

She knew he was lost in thought, voicing his ideas, possibly momentarily unaware of her presence. She knew better than to interrupt. Such a monologue could be very revealing.

"'Eternal' is better, I think," he went on. "It infers no structure, encompasses all 'time' and perhaps a little more --- past, present, future, what preceded the past, what succeeds the future. All at once in existence. All at once." He came back to the room and cast about until he saw her. "That's what I'm talking about, doc. The eternal is what really exists, not just what we define as existing. And Doug, Robert, Martha, Andrew --- they're all parts of the real me, not just the part others define as me. I'm not just Gregory Exeter. I am eternal."

Megalomania? Dr. Stuart thought. Perhaps he was losing his grip on reality and replacing it with one of his own invention. One question should touch that possibility, expose its core. "And what about God? How does God fit into that?"

"What about God?" he repeated, turning the question

over in his mind. "He is eternal, the Creator of all things ---"

"But, if you are eternal..."

Exeter's eyes widened and he looked sharply at her. "I don't believe I'm God, if that's what you're trying to say."

Dr. Stuart nodded encouragingly. "Good, good."

He snorted. "I'm trying to carry on a discussion with my analyst," he mumbled. "Of course, she'll analyze everything to death. Why should she listen?"

"Greg, it's my job."

"I know, I know," he waved her defense away. Sighing, he passed a hand through his hair. "It's just, I have no one to talk to. I'm a bachelor, living alone. My job keeps me traveling, so I haven't time for a social life. Hell, I barely make it to these appointments with you." He lapsed again into silence.

"Couldn't it be that the voices are simply substitutes for the companions you lack on the outside?" she suggested at last.

He thought about that for just a second. "If the voices are internal, doesn't that still mean they're me?"

She was caught short at that. "I don't think that answers my question," she scolded.

"But it does."

She saw that Exeter wasn't disposed to continue that line of reasoning and felt she might have entertained his delusion too long. She might have lost him altogether, but certainly could expect little fruitful exchange now. Looking at her watch, she noticed with dismay there were still more than twenty minutes of the session to go. Worse, he had seen her steal the glance at the time.

"Should we stop for the day, doc?"

She sat down at the desk and put her chin in her hand, elbow on the tabletop. He watched her for a moment, then his eyes wandered toward the window.

"What's out there?" she wanted to know. "You keep looking out the window. Are you looking for something?"

He blinked and shook his head. "I guess you could say I was looking at something."

"What's that?"

"Doug told me he passed after falling from a window."

She worried her pen in her hands. "Doug? But, isn't Doug supposed to be in your future?"

Exeter nodded, never taking his eyes from the window. Dr. Stuart regarded him silently. It would make a kind of sense, she supposed. She had assumed Doug was a living person in a kind of telepathic link to Exeter --- in his delusion, of course. Once again, making assumptions had put her behind the curve. He was ahead of her.

"It's a little weird," he nearly whispered, "knowing that, looking at the window. I wonder if ---" He gasped suddenly, and she saw him grab the arms of his chair as if startled.

"Yes?"

Exeter turned a face bright with sudden enlightenment to her. He fairly beamed. "I know now why the voices talk to me, doc. I know why, of all the manifestations of my eternal being, I was picked to hear them."

A sudden dread filled her and a chill ran along her spine. She swallowed. "And why is that, do you think?" she asked in as steady a voice as she could muster.

He was pulling away from her now, mentally and physically. His voice deepened in timber as he spoke, echoing oddly in the office. "People who have near-death experiences talk about the bright light, the sense of peace they encounter. I understand that now. I feel that."

She clutched her pen until her knuckles whitened and her jaw dropped at what she saw.

Exeter was transforming.

A pale blue light grew around him, forming an aura that flickered, then glowed stronger. The thick black hair whitened until it flowed around his head like a halo of snow. His eyes, burning with a calm yellow flame, found the window as he rose and wafted toward it. Dr. Stuart, stunned, sat helplessly, unable to believe what she knew she was seeing.

"Doug isn't supposed to die that way, doc," Exeter's voice came to her, reverberating subliminally in her mind. The conversational tone of the words contrasted to the supernatural vision. "I am." There was no fear in this assertion. It was a simple statement of fact, made in the same tone one might remark about the weather. "But by doing this, I ensure that my eternal being will reach its goal."

The question rose in her mind unbidden, but before she could utter it, he answered.

"To reach out and touch God, to find Perfection, to attain the Ultimate." His eyes seemed to reach into her soul, resonating against something that quickened under their scrutiny. In that instant, she felt more vulnerable than she had ever been. He was inside her mind, not an invader, but an observer. He took in everything she was in a glance, understood her in a depth at once inhuman and beneficent. He flashed her that quick smile. "Nirvana, if you will. I am so close. Just the awareness of that closeness is so sweet --- "

She almost cried out as he stepped through the window and disappeared.

The quiet that was left in the room settled slowly as she tried to adjust to what had happened. She shook her head and looked around. Exeter was gone, that much was certain. How much else she had actually seen in the last few seconds, she wasn't sure. She stumbled to the window and leaned out. On the pavement in the alleyway six floors below she could see Exeter's broken body. She clasped a hand over her mouth and turned away, closing her eyes to shut out the image.

"Do not mourn for him," a voice whispered in her ear.

Her eyes popped open and she snapped around, looking for the source of the voice. She was alone in the room.

"Hello, Ellen," the voice came again. She felt it just behind her ear, knew it was impossible, but could not stop it. "My name is Rachel."

Dr. Stuart began to scream.

Onorora
Daniel Paton

-Murewa, Zimbabwe-

Nashe had a strange sensation as he walked back from the well on the outskirts of his village. There was something about the hut that called for his attention. Time stood still next to the 7-year old boy who was rooted to the cracked ground, staring.

There was nothing strange about it's appearance - just a normal, mud-walled home with a pointed straw roof. Yet, it gave Nashe an unusual feeling in his stomach and made his head feel heavy. Instinctively, he reached up and rubbed the large birthmark which characterised his smooth head.

The thought that he was going to be late home and his mama would be angry suddenly dawned on him, bringing him out of his daze. He headed back home along the dried and dusty roads as quick as he could without spilling too much of the water that he carried awkwardly in a large, worn bucket.

This was his first time he had been sent to the well on his own and he needed to prove that he was capable and grown up enough to do it. His little legs did their best to carry him the last stretch home, through the scattered farming village which lay in the shadow of imposing mountains. The peaks were visible for leagues around, and punctuated an otherwise flat and desolate land.

Samukele, Nashe's mother, saw her son approaching as she prepared the maize for dinner. She thought she would be angry with him for being so late, but when he finally returned, it was only relief that swept over her. He looked so small against the sparse landscape. If only they were wealthy and lived in town, he wouldn't have to start helping out at such a young age - he could concentrate on playing and learning without a worry. 'Mama, Mama...' He panted as he arrived at her feet. 'Sorry I'm late.'

'It's okay Nashe.' She put the bucket to one side and

hugged him. 'It's okay.'

But something seemed wrong with her son. He seemed weak and his big brown eyes were filled with concern.

'What's the matter?'

He paused, considering whether to mention the feeling he had at the edge of the village - a feeling which still lingered within him.

'I'm tired mama, can I sleep?'

'Of course, but dada will want you up when he comes back from work.'

Nashe managed to drift off in the corner of the room, lying on a few blankets his mama had knitted him before he was born.

He dreamed he was stood back at that spot, gazing at the hut, but it seemed to look smaller now. The sky was a whirling grey abyss above, and the world surrounding the blurry scene didn't exist. Looking down, he realised he was holding the bucket full of water, but it wasn't as heavy as it had felt earlier. It then dawned on him that he wasn't in a 7-year old boy's body anymore; his shell was that of a fully grown man.

A figure appeared in the doorway, waving it's arms around manically, making utterances he did not understand. One hand was clutching something. Intrigued, but with a growing sense of fear, he edged forwards.

It became clear what it was holding far too late: an axe. Before he could even let out a scream, it crashed down on him.

'Nashe!' His father called him back to consciousness. 'Wake up, it's time to eat.'

Dinner consisted of the usual sadza, which Dumiso and Samukele shoveled down gratefully. Nashe, however, couldn't bring himself to consume the meal, instead pushing the mushed-up maize from side to side with his wooden spoon. The images from the dream were still far too vivid, as was the the splitting pain of the axe meeting his skull.

It wasn't just a nightmare. He'd had nightmares before and they just left temporary images in his mind, but this gave him a long-lasting physical feeling of unease.

Night after night he was forced to endure the dream, each time understanding the situation he was thrust into a bit more. He would involuntarily argue with the man, though he could not understand what about. That argument always ended with his murder. The images also were becoming less clouded - one time it was all so clear that he could even see his own reflection in his assaulter's eyes; it was a familiar face, not so different from his father's.

Nashe began to believe that something bad was going to happen, but how could he explain it all to his parents? He could get to the bottom of this himself, after all, he was big enough to fetch water on his own. He was old enough to handle responsibility.

It was time to enter the hut.

However, the next day, on the way to the well, his body rejected his mind's will. Fear paralysed him, and it wasn't long before he gave up and continued his routine journey for water. Tears swelled in his eyes as he lumbered home feeling defeated, dragging the bucket behind him. Once he arrived and sat down, his tired body quickly allowed him to slip into the subconscious. He switched from his own body to that of the man he was used to inhabiting in these visions, and in doing so, he found himself lying down under ground looking up at a roof of mud. There was a gaping hole at the top of his head from which his brains had leaked out and all he wanted was to *get out*, to be *free*, to be *found*....

'Nashe!' His father's face appeared in front of him. 'Wake up Nashe, you're ok. You're safe...'

His mother was lurking behind, looking on with concern. 'You've been having these terrors for weeks, what's going on?'

'He's just a child, he doesn't know....'

'I need to tell you something,' Nashe interrupted.

'Listen to me!' Samukele pleaded to her husband, 'dreams are not always *just* dreams. I've told you before that my mother had visions!'

Their son had fallen asleep again, so they had stepped

outside to discuss what he had just come out with.

'Yes you've said that...'

'So don't you believe me?!'

Dumiso hesitated. 'I believe you, I'm just...'

'Well then! What's the harm in getting a seer to come and-'

'Come and what? What do they really *do*?'

'They can see if he's connected to the spirit world like they are!'

'How about this, I'll go to the place he's on about and check it out for myself?'

She considered this for a moment. 'It could be dangerous.'

'But it might not be.'

***

Dumiso trudged through the sparse landscape. Night was pushing away the last traces of day, leaving the landscape a hazy, blue-tinted grey. It was better to just do this and clear up the whole matter so his wife would calm down, at least his son would then see that dreams *were* just dreams. The superstitions and beliefs of the local totemism culture had always surrounded him but he had little faith in them, instead being much more concerned with the solid, practical things that made up daily life.

His son tottered along at his side - Nashe had been distraught at the idea of not being there. Determined to show his son that nothing was going on, he agreed to bring him along.

They approached the hut they sought and saw a man sat outside the door gazing into the distance. Once he saw them, he jumped with shock and hastily stumbled inside.

A sense of dread was swelling within Nashe and his head started to hurt more than it had before.

'Ay,' Dumiso called out, 'come outside please, can we talk?'

There was no response.

'Come out, I don't mean trouble.'

The man reappeared, now holding a short axe in his right hand. 'What brings you shouting to my home?'

'My son...has had a...vision.' The word stuck in his

throat. 'I've come to clear things up.'

'And what *vision* is this?' He sneered and motioned towards the child with his weapon.

'He says,' Dumiso faltered before deciding just to be straight. 'He says that you killed someone.'

'What?!'

'He thinks...you murdered someone.'

The man looked at Nashe, who was silently staring back, before nervously laughing.

'Well...don't worry, I haven't. So you can go back now, and take your imaginative little boy with you.'

'Round the back.' Nashe said.

'What?!'

'Round the back of the hut is where it is.'

His father looked down at him, seeing his distress and feeling like it was too late to back out of this situation. 'Do you know exactly where?'

'Yes.'

The 7-year-old boy fought against the searing pain in his head and grabbed his father's hand.

'Can we please just take a look in your backyard, to put his mind at ease?'

'No, get away from here!'

Dumiso anxiously let his son lead him forwards.

'Please? I know it seems silly, but...'

'Get away!' He waved the axe around in panic.

Nashe stared at the man who was now shouting things he did not understand, this scene was very familiar.

Before he could say anything, the man raised his weapon above his head and aimed a strike at Dumiso, who managed to dodge out of the way and push Nashe to one side.

'Stop! What are you doing?!'

Again the axe swiped through air but missed it's target. Dumiso waited for the next attempt before countering, grabbing the man's arm mid action and striking his body.

'Please... Calm down!'

The man sent a knee back in reply and fought against Dumiso's grip, who started to panic as the blade edged closer towards him.

His child helplessly screamed as the weapon dragged across his torso.

Shocked, Dumiso stumbled back as blood crept out of the cut, the pain growing by the second.

But the wound was not deep enough to stop him, in fact it gave him the drive needed to finish the fight. A well aimed kick brought his attacker to his knees, a following swipe sent the axe to the ground and a final punch to the face rendered him unconscious.

'Dada!' Nashe ran to his father, and clung onto him.

'This better not have been for nothing!' Dumiso patted the injury, which on examination was little more than a bad scratch. 'Show me where it is.'

They walked to the other side of the small, simple structure and headed through the lightly-fenced field. A dying tree stood in the centre, it's thin branches reaching up like fingers trying desperately to grasp the sky. It was a good place to tie the useless assailant to before he woke up, so Dumiso rushed back to the hut and found some rope.

Meanwhile, Nashe paced ahead, rubbing his birthmark, trying to make the pain stop. His eyes were clouding over but he could see clearer than ever before. He manoeuvred around the thin trunk and stopped dead in his tracks a few steps later.

'Here.'

The patch was less cracked than the ground surrounding it, and felt as though it would give way easier.

Dumiso caught up and at his son's insistence began digging with his hands. Nashe looked on with certainty. A smell of stale rot flew out and it wasn't long before they happened upon something - a dirty white rib.

Another followed, and another, and then Dumiso felt an unmistakable shape.

It was a skull, with a thick crack on the top that sent thin ripples across the rest of it. The shape of the gulf was very familiar and he immediately turned to his child, whose birthmark ceased to hurt.

Silence, Solitude, and A Dark Night
Debasish Mishra

The hands of the clock are the only movements
at this hour and the tick-tock, the only noise.
Everything is still, silent, sinister—
as if my room has swallowed a cemetery.
Sleep refuses to let me into her mansion
of extravagant rooms and I keep knocking the door.
Nobody opens. Nobody responds.
A cold hand sneaks out of nowhere
and touches me, teases me, tinkers with
my peace. A presence but not a presence,
a shadow without a body, an echo, a voice,
a hand bereft of a shoulder, a head and a torso,
a nocturnal intangible nothingness.

The Secret of the Dragon Cabinet
Malina Douglas

It didn't seem strange to her, at first.

Annabelle pressed her cheek to the window as the suburbs of Exeter gave way to long sloping hills. Her mother drove with mounting caution as the road narrowed. Her brother Tommy counted livestock from the back seat. As the car juddered up hills and plunged down steep dips, Annabelle's heart quickened. She heard the familiar crunch of gravel and braced herself to spring out. On the steps of the sprawling white house stood a figure in black with arms extended like wings.

"Auntie Vi," cried Annabelle and Tommy as they burst from the car.

"Hello, Vivienne," said Annabelle's mother in a cordial tone. With a kiss on each child's forehead, she began the drive back. It did not strike Annabelle as odd that her mother never stayed—she was used to it simply being that way.

Aunt Vivienne greeted the children in a voice rich and worn as the wood of the dining room table.

She wore flowing clothes in deep blues and blacks and purples, large necklaces studded with gemstones and long dangling earrings. As usual, she was draped in a black crochet shawl made of loops with large gaps and hanging with many tassels. It was warm and woolly and wrapped around Annabelle when she hugged her, so that she felt as if she were being enveloped in the wings of a great black crow.

The children ran inside. Annabelle loved to explore the large old house, with its creaking floors and heavy curtains framing views of fields.

When Annabelle was eight and her world was small, she thought that all old ladies had collections of ostrich feathers and African beads and baked curious things with strange names. Toad in the hole, Scotch eggs and stargazey pie—a bit frightening because she made the fish heads poke out as if they were trying to escape. Foods not only strange but also wonderful emerged from her cavernous kitchen—eccles cakes filled with spices and dried fruits, sticky Yorkshire parkin, and bread and butter pudding. If the children were naughty they got jellied eels, which were always served cold.

Aunt Vivienne had odd triangular-shaped vessels that she used to make Moroccan *tagine*. There was something magical, it seemed to Annabelle, in the way the spices and vegetables fused together.

"Is this alchemy?" she'd asked, a topic of recent discussion.

Aunt Vi laughed her warm buttery laugh and said, "I suppose you could call it that."

Whenever Annabelle and her brother came to Aunt Vivienne's, they stayed in the Children's Room. Aunt Vi had never had children of her own but she kept it for Annabelle and Tommy. Annabelle loved the upstairs room with its pale blue walls, two single beds bearing bedspreads of jungle scenes, and stuffed animals on each (they fought over the penguin.) There were dinosaurs on the window ledge, a shelf of toy cars on the wall and a big wicker chest full of toys. Tommy would tear into the toys while Annabelle would pull books from the shelf and sit mesmerised, or trace her fingers over the map of Middle Earth, in shades of brown and green and bordered with runes, shimmering faintly if one gazed from a certain direction.

Most of all, she loved the dolls, who sat four in a row on a shelf just above Annabelle's reach. She had to drag the toy chest over to take them down. They were clad in frilled skirts and had big staring eyes and little red lips that said nothing. Their hair fell in thick, luxurious ringlets and seemed real. Even more exciting were the cats.

"The Cats," Aunt Vivienne often said as if speaking a noble title, had divided up the house between themselves and ruled with an uneasy truce. Sheebah resided in the downstairs sitting room and padded around it with a queenly air, her large grey-furred bulk swaying slightly as she moved. She had a particular seat, embedded with long grey hairs, where she curled to sleep, but with a wary eye to anyone who crossed the room. Whoever sat there was duly hissed at.

Smoke was black and panther-sleek. She stalked the upstairs and the garden, appearing beside the children at odd times, as if out of nowhere. It seemed as if she knew places the children didn't.

Annabelle and Tommy roamed the house and gardens freely—through the large kitchen where herbs hung drying and pots bubbled, producing strange smells, to the sitting room with a fireplace like a great hungry mouth, to the dining room with its long rounded table and cabinets of crystal. In their games, dinosaurs battled dragons or heroes set off on great quests across the vast house, scaling the brass lamps and swinging from the tassels, sailing across the carpet or getting mired in the fur of the rug.

They wandered through the long sloping gardens of marigolds and foxgloves, clusters of purple-blue hydrangeas, and climbing roses they pretended were dangerous jungle vines. They rolled down the lawns or hunted for fairies in the bottom of the garden. At times, she heard faint laughter but could not find the source of it. She saw flickers of movement on the edges of her vision but when she turned, there was nothing.

The only place they were not allowed was Aunt Vivienne's bedroom.

Once Annabelle watched Smoke leap up the stairs and followed. The door to Vivienne's room was ajar. Smoke slipped in and disappeared. Annabelle stood in front of the door until her curiosity grew so strong, she pushed it open and peeked in. The curtains were drawn, filtering the light and casting the room in a purple glow. There were charts on the wall, of round diagrams with curious symbols, and everywhere beads—hanging in strands, piled in bowls or threaded onto earrings in a dizzying array of shapes. Most intriguing of all was a large, dark wood cabinet. Smoke nuzzled the corner of it and purred. Annabelle walked closer and saw it was carved with dragons—with spiky wings and long undulating tales that curled up at the ends. She tried the door, but it was locked. Hearing footsteps on the stairs, Annabelle darted out, pulled the door closed behind her, and told herself never to go back again.

After that, Annabelle did as she was told.

In the evenings after dinner, they would gather in the sitting room. Aunt Vivienne told stories of how her late husband, Uncle Albert, had flown planes in the War, of the amulet she'd given him that he'd worn through three near-fatal crashes. Or stories of curious happenings in Devon—wailing banshees and bottomless wells. The children gasped and shrieked with fright. Sheebah watched them from her cushion with half-closed, inscrutable eyes.

"Such lovely hair you have," Aunt Vivienne remarked, as she ran her gnarled fingers through Annabelle's ringlets. Annabelle's hair was coppery brown tinged with gold and hung halfway down her back. Aunt Vi brushed her hair every night before bed, sitting on the sofa behind her while Annabelle sat by the fire on the floor. Aunt Vivienne's hair was short, thin and grey and often invisible, as she tended to wrap it in various scarves—silk, sequinned or paisley.

That night, after Aunt Vivienne had combed out her hair but before she had put the brush away, Annabelle noticed it was full of her hair, a big tawny mass of it.

The next morning, when she took the brush out of its cabinet, the hair was gone.

Annabelle felt a curious sensation, as if the events of the day before had been erased.

***

Annabelle was running. She didn't know why, just that things with sharp claws were coming after her, and she had to get away. She pulled open the wooden trap door to the cellar. Ran down the steps and pulled a pile of blankets over her. She heard scratching and heavy thumping. The sickening sound of wooden beams breaking, then of footsteps coming down the stairs—

She woke up.

She pushed back the blankets—they were completely over her head. She was covered with sweat, breathing hard, and thirsty.

Tommy was still sleeping. She crept across the room and turned the brass doorknob as quietly as she could.

The door creaked on its hinges and she looked back with a panic at Tommy, but he had not moved.

She crept down the stairs. In the hallway she stopped. The light from the sitting room was on. The door was partly open and as Annabelle crept forward, she heard Aunt Vivienne's voice. She froze, listening.

"Don't go," she was saying. "Alison."

Silence.

"Oh Alison."

One of her Auntie's friends must be over. But at this time of the night? She pushed the door open to say hello and found Auntie Vi sitting alone.

"Who's Alison," she asked.

Aunt Vi gave a start and looked over. "Gosh, you startled me."

Then her voice turned stern.

"Why aren't you in bed, young lady?"

"I had a bad dream and came down to get some water."

Vivienne's voice softened. "Oh come here, sweetie." She spread her arms, which looked like wings with lots of holes in them, as she was wearing her tasselled shawl. Annabelle came up and let herself be enfolded. Aunt Vi held her close and stroked her long loose curls.

"It's okay dear, nothing's going to get you."

"But you were just talking to someone, where is she?"

"It's nothing to worry your head about. Come, I'll make you a cup of hot milk."

Annabelle slid off her lap and let Aunt Vi guide her into the kitchen, heat up the milk and tuck her into bed. Before she could wonder who was Alison, the milk's effects soon worked and she slipped into a deep and dreamless sleep.

***

Morning sun streamed into the windows and Annabelle

found Aunt Vi at the breakfast table, dressed in a long silk robe with dangling kimono sleeves, cream and patterned with glistening gold dragons. Sheebah sat on the cushion of the chair beside her, just out of arm's reach.

Vivienne hugged Annabelle, kissed her on the top of the head, and said, "How about pancakes for breakfast?"

"Hooray," said Annabelle, and Tommy found her minutes later dusted in flour and stirring a bowl with a long wooden spoon while Auntie Vi floated around her like a bird.

The day unwound as if the events of the night had never happened.

***

Aunt Vi was called away to visit a sick friend. She swooped through the house, searching for her keys until they jingled in her hand.

"I'll be back as soon as I can."

The children watched as her little black car puttered away and turned the corner. Smoke sat perched on the post of the front gate. She hopped down and darted into the garden.

"What should we do now," asked Annabelle, turning to Tommy.

"Pillow fight!" He raced into the house and Annabelle ran in after him. The small squat pillows from the sofas made excellent ammunition, and the bolsters were like long blunted swords.

They threw and whacked and pummeled each other with pillows until the air was thick with feathers and they collapsed on the floor in peals of laughter.

The Cats had long since been driven away so Tommy jumped onto Sheebah's cushion.

"I wouldn't do that, if I were you," warned Annabelle.

"Says who," replied Tommy. "We can do whatever we want!"

A flash of an idea caught in Annabelle's mind. "Let's play dress-up!" She longed to try on Aunt Vivienne's glittering scarves and silk robes.

"Dress-up's for girls," countered Tommy.

"Not only! There are boy-models too!"

"Oh, all right!" He trailed after Annabelle as she raced up the stairs to Aunt Vi's room.

The door was locked.

"Oh that's annoying," said Annabelle with a huff.

"I know where the key is," said Tommy

"How," said Annabelle. She looked at him with suspicion.

"Because she hangs them all up in the passageway to the barn. I'll show you."

They stamped down the stairs and opened a door in the hall. The passage was dark and seemed to Annabelle like a forbidden cave. One side was lined with books, and the other was a rough stone wall. She wanted to run out and return to the sun and the light of the garden, but Tommy said, "Look."

High up on the stone wall were rows of keys, each hanging on a hook. They were labelled. "Front door," "back door", "airing cupboard", "crystal cabinet", and the last one, with a single letter "V". He snatched it up.

"And this one." It was long and ornate, with knobbly ends and patterned with scales.

"I think this is the key to her wardrobe."

"Could be," said Annabelle, surprised at Tommy's cunning.

The key to the room turned smoothly. They approached the dragon cabinet. Annabelle felt a mix of dread and awe.

She took out the large brass key out of her pocket and unlocked the door. It creaked. She gazed at the row of clothes—two-tone silk robes that changed colours in the light, long beaded skirts, and clothes she had never seen before—a polka dot dress with a flaring skirt, a red velvet jacket with rows of brass fittings, and something short, curved and ribboned that she later learned was a corset.

Tommy wound a scarf around his head. "I'm the maharajah of Devon!" He declared.

As Annabelle turned to the far right, a sight made her freeze. There, pinned to the inside of the cabinet door, were bunches of hair. Long, tawny and golden-tinged hair. Curling hair, and each group of strands had been wound around the head of a pin.

"My hair!" Exclaimed Annabelle.

"Eew, gross!" said Tommy. "Will you tie on my belt?"

But Annabelle was already halfway down the stairs.

***

One evening, Aunt Vi invited dinner-guests. At the door appeared a lady in a filmy blue dress with her hair piled high and a gentleman with a little pointed goatee in a suit jacket.

Aunt Vivienne served cheese-stuffed red peppers with a surprising kick. She lifted a triangular lid to reveal a sizzling *tagine*. They talked about geomancy, dowsing and other things that didn't make sense.

Aunt Vi sent the children to bed but Annabelle soon slipped out again. She sat at the top of the stairs, dark except for a faint glow from the dining room. She listened to Aunt Vi's warm rich voice, the woman's high melodious voice, and the man's ringing bass. She heard the sound of glasses clinking, and laughter, and the woman even sang —in a voice like the flowing of a stream, that carried Annabelle to far away lands. Her eyes felt thick and heavy by the time Aunt Vi kissed the cheeks of her guests and closed the door behind them. Annabelle heard their car crunch away down the gravel drive, then humming.

She seized her chance.

She found Aunt Vi at the kitchen sink, washing out wine glasses, her cheeks flushed.

"What are you doing up?"

"I can't sleep," lied Annabelle.

Aunt Vi put down the wine glasses and rinsed her soapy hands. "Did our noise keep you up?"

"It did."

She wiped off her hands and scooped Annabelle into her arms. "I'm sorry, sweetie. Would you like me to tell you a story?"

"Yes. A story about Alison."

Aunt Vi stiffened.

She put down Annabelle very slowly, so that she slid onto the floor. She pressed both hands on the marble counter and leaned forward, gazing into the window. It was dark outside, so only the reflection of her own face could be seen. She sighed.

"Since you're so very curious... well, it can't be helped."

"What do you mean, Auntie?"

But Vivienne wouldn't answer. She wore an expression Annabelle had never seen. A strange, fierce determination. She seized Annabelle's hand, grabbed a torch from a drawer and led her out through the kitchen door to the garden and up the slope. The hedges and the garden beds seemed shaggy and shadowy, pressing in around them. She caught a glimpse of a cupid's face, pale and ghostly. A shadow moved and she froze.

It solidified into a small black form. Smoke. Annabelle breathed with relief and kept walking. The cat followed.

Foxgloves loomed up like long spindly shadows, higher than Annabelle's head. Aunt Vi's clenched Annabelle's so tightly it hurt.

A wall of shadow loomed up and they passed through a gap in the hedge to a corner of the garden that Annabelle had not known was there. Beneath a yew tree with low hanging boughs and dark bristles, Vivienne stopped. She knelt on the ground beside a rounded stone draped with a wreath, and Annabelle thought, *no, it can't be,* but it was.

"This is where Alison lives now." Her voice sounded rough as a cat's tongue.

"But who was she?"

Aunt Vivienne's voice went quiet, and Annabelle couldn't believe the words she spoke. "She was my daughter. The room you're staying in used to be hers."

"But—I thought you never had any children!"

"I couldn't bear to speak of her. Not since—"

"So are those her dolls?"

"They are."

"But—what happened to her—"

Vi shook herself as if coming awake. "It's cold out here. And you, in bare feet—you'll catch a chill if you stay out. Come."

She took Annabelle's hand and led her back to the house.

From the top of the wall, Smoke watched them, jumped

down, and was gone.

On the stove, Vivienne boiled a pot of milk, and dropped in cinnamon and cloves. "She loved the garden," she said in a soft choked voice. She would plunge her nose into all of the roses in reach. She filled her pockets with fallen petals."

Vivienne tipped in turmeric powder and stirred until the milk became golden.

"She was beautiful, my Alison. With long golden hair that fell in soft curls."

"Is that why you collect my hair," asked Annabelle.

Vivienne turned and gave her a sharp look. "How did you know?"

"I... uh.... saw the strands you hung up..." She twisted her fingers behind her back.

"You've opened my cabinet!"

Annabelle lowered her head down, muttered "Yes." Her body tensed, waiting for the flares of anger to come. They didn't.

Aunt Vi sighed. "I supposed it doesn't matter now." She flicked off the stove and filled up two mugs from the pot. "Come."

She walked through an arched doorway into the sitting room and set down the mugs on the hearthstone. She lit a fire in the hearth and they sat on the carpet beside it.

"You remind me of her," admitted Vi. "I just wanted something when you're not here... something to hold onto."

"But—what happened to her?"

Vivienne sat very straight, gazing into the flames. "I was in the front of the garden, painting. I forgot that the back door was open. I never heard her cries for help. By the time I came outside it was too late. I found her body floating in the pond." Vivienne squeezed her eyes shut and scrunched up her face.

"But there is no pond."

"I filled it in with earth."

Annabelle slid up to Vivienne in silence and embraced her. "I'm sorry," she whispered.

Aunt Vivienne stroked her hair. The fire crackled.

"I drove away my husband with the madness of my grief. I shut myself off from the world."

Annabelle stared in the flames and did not say a word.

"Your mother," began Vivienne, "played a great part in my recovery. She brought me food when I would not feed myself, and she encouraged me to live again. To allow myself to feel joy. I took down all of Alison's pictures and we agreed not to speak of her to anyone. It was better that way."

"I understand..." said Annabelle slowly. "But the paintings... I never saw you paint..."

"I haven't touched a brush since."

They were silent.

Then Annabelle asked, in a small threadbare voice, "Do you think her ghost is still here?"

"She is. I've spoken to her."

Annabelle shivered.

"She's watching over me. She wants to know that I'm okay."

Annabelle wrapped both hands around her mug and took a sip of golden milk.

She leaned against Aunt Vivienne and Vivienne put an arm around her shoulders.

"I was going to make a doll," admitted Vivienne. "Using your hair."

"Oh," shuddered Annabelle. Her stomach lurched and she was gripped by a feeling of revulsion. She wriggled out of Vivienne's grip, out of the room and up the stairs.

"Come back," called Vivienne, but Annabelle shut the door to her room and locked it.

***

Annabelle woke in the middle of the night and sat up. A sound on the edge of her dream had woken her. She glimpsed something silvery on the edges of her vision. She walked through the slumbering house, drawn by a feeling she could not make sense of.

Bare feet lead her over the soft carpet of the sitting room, to the smooth linoleum of the kitchen, and to the garden's cold dirt. She found herself in the secret garden. A bluish-white figure came towards her, a girl. Large plaintive eyes and thick curling hair like her own. Annabelle could see right through her to the shadowy bushes beyond.

"Annabelle," said the girl, stretching out her hand, stroking her hair with translucent fingers.

Annabelle jumped back. "What do you want?"

"To take over your body and see through your eyes!" The girl floated up to her, reaching towards her, into her.

Annabelle felt an icy brush of fingertips. She screamed. She turned and ran, back down the path, and back in through the kitchen door without daring to look behind her. She dove into bed and pulled the blankets over her, wriggling her cold feet, heart racing too fast to sleep.

***

Annabelle followed her mother's brisk footsteps across the gravel drive to the car. She turned around one last time to look. She wished she hadn't.

Smoke stretched from her perch on the wall, turned her back on the children and strutted away. In the doorway stood Vivienne, swathed in layers of shawls, Sheebah circling her ankles. Vivienne's eyes were large and mournful. Annabelle knew now that beneath the layers was a thin, frail woman, lonely and aching.

They turned a corner and she was gone.

It was only much later that the words came. She should have said 'you don't need a doll. You have me,' but instead she had let the revulsion and fear take over her and drive her away from Aunt Vi.

She cut off her hair. Watched the curls pile up at her feet. She hacked off the rest of her name; became Elle. Gave up her dolls to catch toads and climb trees with the boys.

Strange things made her sad: garden ponds and silk scarves, clove-infused milk and anything carved with dragons.

Ophiuchus
Januário Esteves

On the right rise of the celestial equator Apollo grabs
the serpent's head purifying sins of darkness
in a free acceleration of raptured metempsychosis
that transmits to the soul the secret of the substance
     of the one
by molecular oxygen clouds they curve
in a pentagon of stars whose blue expels energy
changeable cyclic dimming repeated on the link
that involves how a metabolic earthquake drifts
mind-boggling ghosts who live in the oracle
pouring dissonant hours on silent statues
puzzle in slow anthropomorphic decomposition
breaking the clay of everyday life into winged muses
bring healing herbs for men's immortality
ionizing matter in the resurrection of tissues
in an astral capsule that travels beyond the spirit
beyond existence, the indivisible remains.

Russia's Well to Hell

In 1970, having lost the race to the moon, the old Soviet Union decided they would instead be the first to reach the Mohorovicic Discontinuity, the theorized boundary between the mostly solid crust and the magma-filled mantle of the earth.

The project, dubbed the Kola Super Bore Hole (KSPB), was placed in the charge of Yuri Smirnov (d. June 2018), a hero of WWII. The location they chose was near Zapolyarny, a tundra town in Pechengsky District of Murmansk Oblast, Russia, located on the Kola Peninsula near the Norwegian border.

The drilling began in the 23-centimeter-wide hole and continued until 1992, when the temperature at the bottom exceeded 180 degrees Celsius (356 F), far beyond expectations. The hole went down over 40,230 feet and remains the deepest hole in the world. At that depth, the Russian scientists described the rock behaving more like plastic. One of the most surprising finds was that, impossibly, there is actually water 7.4 miles down. Research at the site continued until 2006 when funding ran out. The hole was officially abandoned and capped off in 2008, but Smirnov continued to oversee it until his death.

Those are the facts behind the KSPB, but there is more to the story.

According to legend originating sometime around 1989, the hole was in Siberia and actually went down 9 miles before the drill spun free, as if it had reached an opening. In this version of the story, a Mr. Azzacov was in charge of the dig and he ordered heat-resistant microphones and measuring equipment dropped into the hole. They discovered the temperature at the bottom was more than 2000 F, melting the equipment within seconds. The astonished researchers surmised they had reached Hell in the center of the Earth. To support this tale, in 2002 someone produced a tape of sounds purported to be of voices from Hell itself. This tape, probably adapted from soundtrack of the Italian movie *Baron Blood* (1972), has been extensively copied and can be heard on YouTube today. The tape was grabbed up by the Christian Trinity Broadcasting Network and touted as "Scientists Discover Hell." They maintained the information was received from a Finnish newspaper called *Ammennusatia*, but that is actually a religious publication, not a newspaper. Following the popularity of this story, another circulated that something sinister, either a glowing gas plume or even a bat-winged demon, had risen from the hole, sending people scurrying in fear. The demon even wrote "I have conquered" in flames in the sky.

Legend comes from a kernel of truth and expands as time goes by. It becomes more and more difficult to separate fact from fantasy because people love stories, especially if those stories challenge their ideas about the mundane nature of the world. Russia's Well to Hell is a perfect example of this kind of challenge.

REFERENCES

Edwards, Charlotte. "World's Deepest Manmade Hole Dubbed 'Well to Hell' PLUNGES 40,000 Feet." *New York Post*, New York Post, 28 Aug. 2019, nypost.com/2019/08/27/worlds-deepest-man-made-hole-dubbed-well-to-hell-plunges-40000-feet/.

IMDb. "Baron Blood." *IMDb*, IMDb.com, www.imdb.com/title/tt0069048/trivia/?ref_=tt_trv_trv.

Mallonee, Laura. "Inside the Post-Soviet Towns Built around A 40,000-Foot Hole." *Wired*, Conde Nast, 31 Mar. 2016, www.wired.com/2016/03/inside-post-soviet-towns-built-around-40000-foot-hole/.

Smith, Jodi. "The Legendary 'Well to Hell' Is a
    Russian Borehole Said to Be Filled with Screaming,
    Tormented Souls." *Ranker.com*, Ranker, 1 Apr.
    2020, www.ranker.com/list/about-russian-well-to-
    hell/jodi-smith.

Wiles, Jamie. "The Fascinating Truth behind the 'Well to
    Hell' Hoax." *Urbo*, 17 Aug. 2020,
    www.urbo.com/content/the-fascinating-truth-
    behind-the-well-to-hell-hoax/.

Yurenev, Alexey. "YURI'S Journey to Hell." *Yurenev*,
    Squarespace, 2020, www.yurenev.com/yuris-
    journey-to-hell.

You are a little soul carrying around a corpse.
– Epictetus –

Edison's Forgotten Spirit Phone

Thomas Alva Edison had many inventions attributed to him including the phonograph and the light bulb, but most people are unaware of the most bizarre of his invention ideas: the "spirit phone."

It was 1920, and the world was still reeling from the losses of the Great War. Many families had suffered deaths of loved ones and the thought of being able to speak with them caught the imagination of the world. Psychic mediums were having a heyday and charlatans bilked thousands out of their life savings preying on the need to talk to loved ones gone.

But why would such a down-to-earth businessman and inventor even consider such a radical idea?

In the middle 1800s, three sisters in New York declared they had made contact with a being from the afterlife named Mr. Splitfoot. They became an immediate sensation, fascinating dignitaries as famous as Sir Arthur Conan Doyle with their exploits. Even their admission in 1888 that they had faked the effects did nothing to quell the excitement around the new movement that became known as Spiritism.

The possibility of being able to talk with the dead brought the attention of many thinkers of the age including Alexander Graham Bell. His brother Edward, who died at the age of 19, and he made a pact that whoever died first would try to communicate from the Other Side. It is said that Bell's invention of the telephone was inspired by his attempts to do just that. Guglielmo Marconi, in his work with radio, was convinced that it could be done, even sketching out plans for a spirit phone himself (Nugent 2019).

But it wasn't until two of the finest minds of the 20th century tackled the idea that things really became well-known.

Nicola Tesla and Thomas Edison began as employee and employer but eventually became bitter rivals. Tesla, in his work with electrics, had heard odd sounds coming from his equipment early on, and even wrote:

> "My first observations positively terrified me, as there was present in them something mysterious, not to say supernatural, and I was alone in my laboratory at night... The sounds I am listening to every night at first appear to be human voices conversing back and forth in a language I cannot understand. I find it difficult to imagine that I am actually hearing real voices from people not of this planet. There must be a more simple explanation that has so far eluded me. " (qtd by Debczak 2019)

Of course, what Tesla was listening to we would now characterize as "white noise" that can mimic the sounds of incoherent human speech or other noises. But the fact that Tesla might have found something spurred Edison into action.

In his own words in an October 1920 issue of *The American Magazine*:

> "If our personality survives, then it is strictly logical or scientific to assume that it retains memory, intellect, other faculties and knowledge that we acquire on this Earth. Therefore, if personality exists after what we call death, it is reasonable to conclude that those who leave the

Earth would like to communicate with those they have left here. I am inclined to believe that our personality hereafter will be able to affect matter. If this reasoning be correct, then, if we can evolve an instrument so delicate as to be affected by our personality as it survives in the next life, such an instrument, when made available, ought to record something." (qtd by Armstrong 2012)

"I have been at work for some time building an apparatus to see if it is possible for personalities which have left this earth to communicate with us." (qtd by Wagner 2019)

A little later, he qualified his previous statement when speaking to *The Scientific American*:

"I have been *thinking* for some time of a machine or apparatus which could be operated by personalities which have passed on to another existence or sphere... This apparatus is in the nature of a valve, so to speak. That is to say, the slightest conceivable effort is made to exert many times its initial power for indicative purposes...

"I don't claim that our personalities pass on to another existence or sphere. I don't claim anything because I don't know anything about the subject. For that matter, no human being knows. But I do claim that it is possible to construct an apparatus which will be so delicate that if there are personalities in another existence or sphere who wish to get in touch with us in this existence or sphere, the apparatus will at least give them a better opportunity to express themselves than the tilting tables and raps and ouija boards and mediums and the other crude methods now purported to be the only means of communication...

"I believe that if we are to make any real

progress in the psychic investigation," he said, "we must do it with scientific apparatus and in a scientific manner, just as we do in medicine, electricity, chemistry, and other fields." (qtd by Wagner 2019; Tablang 2019; Tapalaga 2020)

Edison considered human life to be more than just an individual experience. Wagner again quotes him:

> "There are many indications that we human beings act as a community or ensemble rather than as units. That is why I believe that each of us comprises millions upon millions of entities, and that our body and our mind represent the vote or voice, whichever you wish to call it, of our entities.... The entities live forever.... Death is simply the departure of the entities from our body...
>
> "I do hope that our personality survives. If it does, then my apparatus ought to be of some use. That is why I am now at work on the most sensitive apparatus I have ever undertaken to build, and I await the results with the keenest interest." (Wagner)

Edison supposedly went so far as to call together scientists, mediums, and psychics for an experiment held in his laboratory using light shone on a photoelectric cell, according to a 1933 article in *Modern Mechanix*. He posited that, during a séance, if there actually were a spirit present, the light would be interrupted and that would register on the cell's output. Although the fact of this meeting and its outcome is considered by many to be urban legend, the story persists to this day (Debczak; Martin, et al 2017)

Many consider the whole thing to have been a hoax, that Edison was having the newspapers and magazines on about it. No blueprints, notes, or prototype of the device ever turned up until a French journalist named Philippe Baudouin, browsing a Parisian thrift store in 2015, found a rare copy of Edison's diary. In it are supposed to be Edison's thoughts on the afterlife and actual plans for a spirit phone (Nugent).

Perhaps the documents now found will enable the design and build of an actual device to speak with the departed. Only time will tell.

REFERENCES

Armstrong, Thomas. "Thomas Edison's Telephone to the Afterlife." *The American Institute for Learning and Human Development*, 21 Aug. 2012, https://www.institute4learning.com/2012/08/21/thomas-edisons-telephone-to-the-afterlife/.

Debczak, Michele. "When Thomas Edison Tried Besting Nikola Tesla by Building a 'Spirit Phone.'" *Mental Floss*, 25 Oct. 2019, https://www.mentalfloss.com/article/602456/thomas-edison-nikola-tesla-spirit-phone.

Martin, Joel, and William J. Birnes. "Who You Gonna Call?: Edison's Science of Talking to Ghosts." *Salon*, Salon.com, 8 Oct. 2017, https://www.salon.com/2017/10/08/who-you-gonna-call-edison-and-the-science-of-talking-to-ghosts/.

Nugent, Addison. "The Great Inventors Who Really Wanted to Talk to Ghosts." *OZY*, 8 Nov. 2019, https://www.ozy.com/true-and-stories/the-greatest-turn-of-the-century-inventors-really-wanted-to-talk-to-ghosts/221925/.

Science Staff. "Thomas Edison's 'Lost' Idea: A Device to Hear the Dead." *Phys.org*, Phys.org, 5 Mar. 2015, https://phys.org/news/2015-03-thomas-edison-lost-idea-device.html.

Tablang, Kristin. "Thomas Edison, B.C. Forbes And The Mystery Of The Spirit Phone." *Forbes*, Forbes Magazine, 28 Oct. 2019, https://www.forbes.com/sites/kristintablang/2019/10/25/thomas-edison-bc-forbes-mystery-spirit-phone/?sh=1842f86129ad.

Tapalaga, Andrei. "Thomas Edison's Invention That Allowed People to Talk to the Dead." *Medium*, History of Yesterday, 31 Dec. 2020, https://historyofyesterday.com/thomas-edisons-invention-that-allowed-people-to-talk-to-the-dead-940a1f12f1f.

Wagner, Stephen. "Edison's Quest to Communicate With the Dead." *LiveAbout*, LiveAbout, 23 Feb. 2019, https://www.liveabout.com/edison-and-the-ghost-machine-2594017.

www.ingramcontent.com/pod-product-compliance
Lightning Source LLC
LaVergne TN
LVHW011842060526
838200LV00054B/4133